"You had no business laying a kiss on me—especially like that!"

Hannah felt herself flushing as he cupped her face. Right or wrong, who cared, when it felt so darn good....

Dylan had started this on impulse. Mostly as a test. Instead, the delectable Hannah Reid kissed as if she was all of sixteen, tentativeness turning to enthusiasm, shy reserve to passion. And it was that mixture of innocence and ardor that was nearly his undoing. It had been so long since he'd felt anything genuine or spent time with anyone this complicated and challenging. And he needed that, he realized. Needed this... unbridled passion.

Unfortunately, because of his suspicions about Hannah, he couldn't give in to it. At least not yet.

Hearts pounding, regrets already forming—on both sides—they drew apart. Hannah looked at him as if she wanted to simultaneously kiss him and smack him for his audacity.

He knew how she felt.

He wanted to kiss her and smack himself, too....

Dear Reader,

It's a well-known fact. Eavesdropping on other people's conversations is not something any of us should be doing deliberately.

But suppose you accidentally stumbled across a family member and a dear friend about to make the biggest mistake of their lives—one that could have ramifications for years to come. Do you stand by and do nothing and live forevermore with the knowledge that you could have prevented tons of heartache, had you only dared to act? Or risk their ire and get involved up to your chin in whatever's going on?

In *Plain Jane's Secret Life,* that's the dilemma presented to Dylan Hart on the night of his sister Janey's wedding when he sees his brother Cal and old friend Hannah Reid in a top-secret rendezvous at The Wedding Inn. Dylan has never been one to meddle in other people's "risky business." But this time he can't help getting involved. Even if circumstances—and the beautiful tomboy's suspicions—demand he do it ever so discreetly...

Meanwhile, talented mechanic Hannah Reid isn't sure what's come over Dylan Hart. She knows the sexy TV sportscaster is secretly weathering his own personal crisis—and she's agreed to help him emerge as victorious as ever—but that doesn't explain his sudden, very intense interest in *her.* Were the two of them falling in love at long last? Or was there something else, something much more curious, going on...?

I hope you have as much fun reading this next book in THE BRIDES OF HOLLY SPRINGS series as I had writing it! And please do visit my Web site www.cathygillenthacker.com for information on my books.

Best wishes,

Cathy Gillen Thacker

Cathy Gillen Thacker

PLAIN JANE'S SECRET LIFE

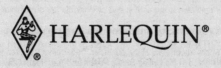

HARLEQUIN®

TORONTO • NEW YORK • LONDON
AMSTERDAM • PARIS • SYDNEY • HAMBURG
STOCKHOLM • ATHENS • TOKYO • MILAN • MADRID
PRAGUE • WARSAW • BUDAPEST • AUCKLAND

ISBN 0-373-75033-1

PLAIN JANE'S SECRET LIFE

Copyright © 2004 by Cathy Gillen Thacker.

This edition published by arrangement with Harlequin Books S.A.

® and TM are trademarks of the publisher. Trademarks indicated with ® are registered in the United States Patent and Trademark Office, the Canadian Trade Marks Office and in other countries.

www.eHarlequin.com

Printed in U.S.A.

Chapter One

"Unbelievable," Hannah Reid muttered to herself as she watched Dylan Hart saunter out of the Raleigh-Durham airport terminal, full entourage in tow. His sister Janey's wedding was in less than an hour, and the handsome TV sportscaster was stopping to sign autographs and shake hands. Okay, so the autographs were to beaming kids, the handshakes to their parents and the two airport security men walking beside Dylan. But still, Hannah fumed as Dylan scanned the area and finally strode quickly over to the Classic Car Auto Repair van she had idling at the passenger pickup lane.

"Where's the Bentley?" Dylan asked, opening the rear door and climbing inside.

Irked that he was treating her more like a chauffeur than an old family friend, Hannah pulled out into the traffic exiting the airport. The least he could have done was issue a personal greeting. *If not climb in the front and ride shotgun beside her.* "Back in Holly Springs. It's being used to transport the bride and groom to and from the ceremony. Speaking of which—"

"Yeah, yeah, I know, I'm running late," Dylan acknowledged cheerfully. "But so from the looks of things are you. Unless you *plan* to participate in the nuptials with grease on your face?"

Hannah touched her hand to her cheek and then rubbed her soiled fingertips on the leg of her denim overalls. Damn. She couldn't believe she had done that again….

"Not to worry." Dylan caught Hannah's eye in the rearview mirror and winked. "I won't tell anyone where you've been."

"Har de har har." With effort, Hannah kept her eyes on the road. She did not need to be noticing how much more handsome Dylan Hart seemed to get every time she saw him. Just because he was super well put together—even today he had traveled in a sleekly attractive business suit and tie—and looked mouthwateringly handsome on the television screen—did not mean she had to go all gaga over him, too.

So what if he had bedroom eyes, a mesmerizingly sexy smile and dimples cute enough to make her sigh out loud? Or expertly cut sandy-brown hair, glowing golden skin and crinkly laugh lines at the corners of his sable-brown eyes? He also had the exceedingly stubborn Hart jaw, and the personality that went with it. Plus a way of standing back and merely observing life, which she found extremely irritating.

"Where have you been?" Dylan continued conversationally as he moved around in the back seat, giving her repeated glimpses of his broad shoulders and sturdy compact body in the rearview mirror.

"Emergency call, working on a vintage Jag," Hannah muttered over the rustle of clothing being pulled out of a carry-on garment bag. One of his masculine, nicely manicured hands accidentally brushed the side of her face. *What was he doing back there?*

More rustling as Dylan sat back slightly and shrugged out of his suit jacket and tie. "Today?"

Hannah knew what he was thinking—she was in this wedding, too. "I had time," Hannah said deferentially while Dylan pulled a shaver out of an expensive leather toiletries bag and began running it over his jaw. "Or I thought I did." She spoke above the buzzing noise of the razor and scowled. "Until your flight was late." Now they were all off schedule. And she would have even less time to put herself together before walking down the aisle—on Dylan Hart's arm!

"Weather delay." Dylan shrugged. He slapped on some deliciously enticing aftershave, moved his head toward the window and peered out at the afternoon sky. "Looks like it's clearing up here, though."

"Finally," Hannah sighed in relief, taking the turn-off to Holly Springs. "After days of rain."

Was that her imagination or was she hearing him undress? "Do you have your seat belt on?" she asked with a frown, telling herself what she was imagining could not be so.

Dylan chuckled and continued to move around behind her on the vinyl seat, much more freely than he should have. "Ah—not at the moment, no."

He sounded distracted.

So was she.

Aware her heartbeat was accelerating and her imagination was soaring even more wildly out of control, Hannah gripped the steering wheel even tighter. She tried not to think about the way her skin had tingled when he had accidentally brushed her face. Hannah reminded primly, "We're on the highway, Dylan!"

Safety, however, seemed the least of his concerns. Dylan moved around all the more. Out of her peripheral vision, Hannah saw the shirt he had been wearing whip past the back of her head and the starched white tuxedo shirt come off its hanger.

"I trust your driving—you having a chauffeur's license and all," Dylan replied lazily, the hard muscles of his chest flexing as he worked his way into the required shirt in the confined space.

Oh, my. Was it getting hot in here or what?

Hannah reached for the AC controls and turned it

to maximum cool as beads of perspiration gathered between her breasts. "Even so..." Hannah reprimanded. She heard another, even more telling zip and whoosh of cloth moving over skin.

"I can't exactly get my pants off with my lap belt fastened," Dylan drawled.

He had to be teasing her. He would not actually be stripping down all the way in her vehicle. Right...?

Hannah glanced over her shoulder, sure she would find she had been imagining things. Instead, her eyes widened at the sinewy chest, visible through the unbuttoned halves of his crisp white shirt, and the sexy lines of his broad, muscular shoulders. At six foot, Dylan Hart might be the shortest of the five Hart brothers, but there was nothing small about him.

Hurriedly Hannah turned her gaze back to the road. Her palms were trembling. Her emotions ran riot. "What are you doing?" she demanded in a strangled voice, trying without success to forget the rest of what she had seen. Long muscular legs. Black silk bikini briefs clinging to...

Never mind what the fabric was molding!

She had a job to do here and that was to get them both to Janey and Thad's wedding!

"SOMEONE NEEDS TO ASK Hannah Reid to dance," Mac Hart said.

Dylan looked at his oldest sibling. Somehow, he

wasn't surprised Mac would be the one to bring this up. Mac had always been the law-and-order member of his family, even before becoming sheriff of Holly Springs some five years prior.

"Yeah," Fletcher chimed in. Having recently discovered romance himself, with florist Lily Madsen, the vet in the family was now into chivalry, big-time. "The reception is almost over and no one has asked Hannah to dance."

"No surprise there," Dylan muttered, looking around for the town's premier mechanic, relieved to find her nowhere in sight. Although Hannah was often reserved in what she had to say—to him, anyway—she had a way of looking at him that made him think she always expected more from him.

"Hannah's like a—" Dylan had been about to say "sister," but that notion had gone out the window the moment he had seen Hannah dolled up in the sexy black-and-white dress, black stockings and heels that his sister Janey had chosen for her bridesmaids.

"—like one of the guys," Dylan finished. Although he'd always thought of her as a "plain Jane," today she had transformed herself into an auburn-haired goddess. How come he'd never noticed her creamy skin and vibrant green eyes before? And it wasn't that Hannah hadn't always had a very remarkable set of curves on her. Just that they were usually hidden beneath a pair of grimy coveralls, or equally shapeless and masculine attire. On the job or off. "The way she is always talking sports and hanging out to drink beer and watch NASCAR and swap stories with the guys and stuff."

"She doesn't really watch NASCAR anymore," Mac interrupted.

"Yeah," the very married Joe Hart chimed in.

Dylan turned to Joe, amazed at the changes in his baby brother. Three months ago, all Joe had cared about was the sport he played. Then he had joined lives with his boss's daughter, Emma Donovan. And now—much to Dylan's aggravation—the pro hockey player considered himself the authority on wedded bliss. When, unbeknownst to all of them, it was really Dylan who had the "score" on that.

"Not since Hannah and Rupert Wallace broke it off," Joe pointed out casually, helping himself to a last slice of wedding cake.

That had been two years ago, Dylan recalled. He glanced around, wondering where his brother Cal was. Since Cal's wife, Ashley, had called to say she wouldn't be coming to the wedding after all—the pretty doctor was stuck in Honolulu, working on her OB/GYN fellowship—Cal had been in a funk and kept mostly to himself.

"And it doesn't matter how much she's one of the guys," Fletcher continued sternly. "She's a bridesmaid. She ought to get at least one dance. And since you're the groomsman who escorted her down the aisle at the church, it's your responsibility."

Dylan tried not to think what it would feel like to hold Hannah Reid's surprisingly soft and feminine-looking body in his arms. Or see that knowing look in her eyes once again. Too much one-on-one time with her and he might do something really foolish—like kiss her.

"All right, all right," he muttered in exasperation, giving in at last, telling himself he could manage to keep his secret desire for her at bay during one brief dance. "Where is she?" He was determined to get this over with as soon as possible.

"Last I saw she was headed upstairs," Mac said.

"To help Janey change into her going-away outfit?" Dylan asked, aware that the groom—Thad—had just come back down to rejoin the two hundred or so guests left in the Wedding Inn ballroom.

His brother shrugged as one song ended and another began. Aware he'd never hear the end of it if he didn't ask the bridesmaid he had been paired with to dance, Dylan headed out into the marble-floored hallway and up the sweeping staircase that led to the second floor.

The door to the bride's changing suite was closed. He could hear laughing female voices emanating from behind it. The groom's changing suite, on the other side of the staircase, was empty. Thrusting his hands in the pockets of his black tuxedo pants, Dylan strolled that way, killing time, as he waited for the women to come out. And that was when he heard it, the voices a little farther down the hall. Coming from the dressing suite usually reserved for the groom's parents.

"Got any tips on dealing with—what's his name again?" Dylan heard Hannah ask.

Curious, and wondering just who she was with, he strolled soundlessly closer.

"R. G. Yarborough," Dylan was stunned to hear his brother Cal reply in a crisp, matter-of-fact voice. "And it's important to start out on the right foot with him," Cal added somewhat impatiently. "So wear a skirt."

Dylan frowned. Did she even have one? Aside from the bridesmaid dress she had worn tonight, and the gowns from the various other weddings she had been in? What was it women said about that? Always a bridesmaid never a bride?

Hannah's beleaguered sigh whispered out into the hall. "What else?" Hannah asked Cal reluctantly.

Trying not to think why his brother—whose own decade-long marriage to his college sweetheart seemed to be having trouble—would be advising one of the most beautiful tomboys in the area who to see or what to wear, Dylan leaned against the wall.

"He's probably going to be difficult," Cal continued advising, as if he was a coach before a game, and Hannah was one of his players. "But if you use all your charm…show Yarborough you really know what you're doing—"

Know what you're doing? Dylan's eyes widened at the various interpretations of that sage and somewhat *sexual*-sounding advice.

"How old is he again?" Hannah interrupted, sounding as if she could barely keep track of the conversation at hand. And no wonder, given the sound of what his brother was asking her to do here! He'd be flummoxed, too.

"Forty-five, fifty, near as I can figure. And married," Cal said, his voice dropping another warning notch. "So—"

"I'll keep that in mind," Hannah promised.

"Good." Cal sounded relieved. When what his orthopedic-surgeon older brother really ought to feel, Dylan thought resentfully, was guilty. Guilty as hell. For arranging anything with Hannah and a married man who was way too old for her. For heaven's sake! Didn't Cal think about the fact that Hannah was not exactly experienced when it came to men? Hell, Dylan couldn't even recall Hannah even dating anyone save that NASCAR driver, Rupert Wallace, if you could even call those dates. Mostly, Dylan recalled the two of them with their heads bent over some car engine…

Hannah, up to her elbows in grease and wrenches…

"So where is this guy going to be?" Hannah asked.

"You're to meet him in an hour at Sharkey's Pool Hall. In Raleigh."

Not the best neighborhood. Or the classiest establishment for a woman to go into. With or without a date.

"If the preliminary goes well, maybe he'll take you back to his house from there."

Preliminary, Dylan fumed, feeling more shocked and incensed than he had in all of his twenty-eight years. *Preliminary what!*

"Yarborough's wife won't mind?" Hannah asked, sounding both concerned and skeptical.

"Out of town." Cal's voice held a dismissive shrug. "She took the kids to California to visit family for two weeks."

Never dreaming what was going on behind her back, Dylan was willing to bet, recalling with chilling accuracy how he had felt when similarly betrayed.

"So basically I've got that amount of time—" Hannah speculated thoughtfully.

There was another pause, rife with meaning.

His curiosity killing him—none of this sounded like the compassionate older brother or the affable mechanic he knew—Dylan hazarded a discreet glance around the open doorway. There were no lights on and the room was shrouded in shadow, but through the semidarkness he could see Hannah with her back to the wall, staring up at Cal. The expression on her face was the same one she wore when she was trying to figure out a particularly thorny mechanical problem on one of the expensive automobiles she worked on at the business she owned, Classic Car Auto Repair. She narrowed her eyes at Cal. "You said the guy is loaded?"

Hands thrust in the pockets of his tuxedo pants, Cal shook his head in disgust. "Yarborough's got so much money he doesn't know what to do with it," he replied in a voice that was equally calculating. Cal took his hands out of his pockets and spread his hands wide. "Which is, of course, part of the problem. Had R. G. Yarborough a little less—"

Hannah nodded in understanding. "You'd be able to deal with him a lot more effectively," she said.

"Right," Cal agreed.

Dylan, wary of being seen, ducked back out of sight again but remained within earshot of the low, urgent voices.

"Well, don't worry. I'm sure I can manage him." To Dylan's mounting dismay, the smile was back in Hannah's voice.

Even as Dylan's brother got grimmer…

"And one more thing, Hannah," Cal warned. "No one, and I mean no one, can know about what we've got going here." His voice caught momentarily. "If Ashley were to get wind of it—"

No joke, Dylan thought, aware what Cal's semi-estranged wife might think. The same thing he was thinking right now.

"I understand completely, believe me," Hannah promised in sweet sincerity. "You don't have to worry for one second, Cal. No one—and I mean no one—is going to hear about this from me."

THE TROUBLE WITH eavesdropping, Dylan thought, was what you thought something meant, might be completely misconstrued. For instance, there was no way Cal was supervising and setting up the twenty-eight year old Hannah Reid's secret nocturnal activity with a wealthy-as-all-get-out man she had never met. And might not, from the sounds of it, even really want to meet under normal circumstances. At least not for socializing.

So here he was, an hour later, getting out of a cab in front of Sharkey's Pool Hall...never having had that dance he was supposed to request from her.

He walked in, not sure what to expect. Hannah was standing by a pool table, a bottle of beer in her hand. She was dressed in a short black skirt, stockings and heels that showed off her spectacular legs. A red knit tank top with a high neck and a racer back clung to her ample breasts, and made her slender shoulders and bare arms look incredibly feminine. A man Dylan assumed was R. G. Yarborough was standing next to her. He was fifty, at least, and attractive in that money-to-burn way. That was if you liked spiked gray-brown hair and an exceptionally hard body that appeared manufactured by steroids, fancy gym equipment and maybe even plastic surgery. Plus his appearance—college T-shirt with the sleeves rolled up, baggy cargo-style jeans and an earring in one ear—practically screamed midlife crisis. All in all, not a good guy for an innocent-in-the-ways-of-the-world woman like Hannah to be tangling with.

Jacket hooked over his shoulder, bow tie hanging undone on either side of the open collar of his pleated white tuxedo shirt, Dylan skirted the large, rectangular hall and numerous pool tables to the long wooden bar along one side. Keeping to the shadows, he approached the bartender and asked for a bottle of light beer.

He leaned against the bar, watching. And he wasn't the only one. A lot of male eyes were on Hannah at that particular second as she set a triangle on the green-felt tabletop. The bartender, included. "Know her?" he asked Dylan.

Dylan nodded, but even as he did he was wondering if he really did. The sexy-as-hell woman in front of him wasn't even close to the lady mechanic and all-around tomboy he recalled growing up with.

"Yeah, well, she hasn't been in here before. I guarantee I'd remember that little filly if she had been," the bartender murmured.

And no wonder. Hannah's pretty face was alight

with feminine mischief and barely reined-in flirtation as she bantered animatedly with the group of men standing around the pool table. Color flooded her face. Her auburn hair was flowing in unruly waves down around her bare shoulders. Every time she moved, her hair brushed her silky-looking skin and drew attention to the sumptuous curves of her breasts. Worse, as she captured another loose ball and fit it into the triangle, the tank top rode above her waist, baring even more silky-smooth skin. Dylan felt a tightening in his groin, and was willing to bet, every other man there did too.

As she straightened, slowly, R. G. Yarborough reached out and stroked a hand along her hip. Hannah tensed visibly but didn't resist as she turned to face him. She murmured something—Dylan couldn't make out quite what—and the rich guy responded by pulling out his wallet and extracting several bills.

Hannah mocked whatever he was offering, but appeared ready to take him up on his proposal.

Normally, Dylan would have remained on the sidelines, no matter what was going on. But this was too much. He didn't know what Cal had gotten the naive Hannah Reid into, but Dylan was for damn sure not going to stand idly by and watch someone he'd known from their elementary-school days get hurt.

He moved away from the bar and sauntered toward the pool table where Hannah was still flirting madly. "Money?" Dylan heard her say as she tucked the bills back into Yarborough's hands. "Come on. Surely—" Hannah batted her eyelashes at him "—you and I can wager for something a little more interesting than that…."

Yarborough looked down at Hannah, a lecherous gleam in his eyes. "Well, maybe we could at that," Yarborough flirted back as Dylan stopped just short of them. Determined to interrupt before this charade went any further, he said casually, "Hey, Hannah."

She looked over and froze, the color draining from her face. Recovering admirably, she said, "Dylan. Fancy meeting you here."

"What's that saying?" Dylan asked, pretending to all those witnessing the scene that he had some claim to Hannah. "Wherever you go-est, I go-est?"

Yarborough looked Dylan up and down, then turned to Hannah and asked, "This your husband?"

Hannah's smile tightened. "No. Most definitely not."

"Boyfriend?" Yarborough persisted.

Dylan clamped a hand around Hannah's shoulders. "Hannah doesn't like the term *boyfriend*," he said. "Too high school. But to answer your question, yes, she and I do go back a ways."

Hannah glared at him in a way that said back off,

then turned back to R.G. "It's not what you think. Dylan's like a brother to me."

"A brother who does not want to see you hurt," Dylan continued, looking at her just as meaningfully.

Hannah propped her hands on her hips as a crowd began to gather round them. She was so piqued with him that steam was practically coming out of her ears. "Since when are you my keeper?" she demanded, even as the two guys nearest them elbowed each other. "Hey," one of them said, taking a closer look at Dylan. "Aren't you that guy that used to be on W-MOL, doing the sports?"

"Yeah. Dylan Hart, isn't it?" someone else asked, edging closer.

"You coming back to work on one of the local TV stations again?" another asked excitedly.

"Yeah," chimed a fourth. "You were good!"

Looking relieved to no longer be the center of attention, Hannah patted Dylan on the arm. "Maybe you should attend to your fan club and let me continue here."

Dylan looked down at her, still not sure what she had been about to wager. He couldn't say why exactly, he just knew he was more certain than ever that she was doing something she did not want him, or anyone else in Holly Springs, to know about. "No way."

Her soft lips took on a mutinous line. "Excuse us,

will you?" Hannah tugged him aside. "What are you doing here?"

"Looking out for you."

She drew a deep breath, clearly exasperated, as she apparently did not want to be kept away from the unsavory types, by him or anyone else. "How did you even know I was here?" she hissed.

Wondering if he would ever in a million years understand women and why they were drawn to rich losers over decent hardworking guys like himself, Dylan replied as if it were the most natural thing in the world, "I followed you from Holly Springs."

That gave her pause, Dylan noted with grim satisfaction. "Why?" she asked a lot more cautiously.

Dylan shrugged, never taking his eyes from her face. This much at least he had been prepared to answer. "You've got my stuff in the van. My carry-on luggage. The clothes I was wearing earlier. It's all in the back."

Yarborough strode over. "Hey, babe," he drawled so lasciviously Dylan wanted to punch his face. "You going to play or not?"

To Dylan's chagrin, Hannah looked torn, as if she wanted to go off with R.G., just not in front of Dylan, or anyone else she knew from Holly Springs.

Not gonna happen, Dylan decided. He winked over at her with a playfulness he knew she would not appreciate. "I don't mind." He shrugged his shoulders lazily. "I can wait."

Hannah dug into the front pocket of her tight black skirt. "I'll just give you the keys and you can go on out and get your stuff." She pressed them into his palm, her fingers warm against his.

Dylan planted his feet firmly beneath him and resisted the way she was practically pushing him away. "I also need a ride back to Holly Springs," Dylan continued matter-of-factly.

Abruptly, Hannah stopped pushing. "I thought you followed me here," she said with a frown.

Dylan examined her keys. "In a cab."

Her pretty pine-green eyes radiated displeasure. "You can't take a cab back?"

Dylan shrugged. "I'm out of cash. But that's okay." He leaned against the pillar at his back, prepared to do whatever it took. "Like I said, I can wait."

Thwarted, Hannah gave up. "Wait here," she commanded furiously as she stalked off, R. G. Yarborough in tow, and said something to him that he looked none too happy to be hearing.

There was another brief exchange. One that Yarborough seemed to be on the losing end of again, then Hannah headed back to Dylan, her strides long and sexy. "You're turning out to be one royal pain today," she told him as they headed toward the door, side by side. "You know that, don't you?"

"So I'll make it up to you," Dylan drawled, wondering how it was that he could have known Hannah

Reid as long as he had and never made a single pass at her.

"How?" Hannah snapped, giving him yet another hot, aggravated look.

Dylan reached past her to open the door. Still determined to find out what was going on with the former tomboy, he smiled at her gallantly. "I'll buy you dinner."

Chapter Two

Hannah stared at Dylan as they moved out onto the sidewalk. He appeared to be serious, anyway. Not that she would in any way consider this to be an invitation for a date. The men she knew from Holly Springs did not ask her out on dates. "When?" she said, still not sure what Dylan Hart was up to this evening.

He shot her another appreciative male glance. "Right now sounds good to me."

Hannah ignored the unsettling way her senses stirred at his proximity. She stepped back a pace, then another. "We already ate at the reception."

He stood, legs braced apart, arms folded in front of him. "That was more like a late lunch. Unless you're used to eating the seniors' special at 4:00 p.m."

"Very funny." She made a face at him, refusing to be charmed by his teasing.

"Come on," he cajoled her, his hot gaze sliding

over her from head to toe before returning with heart-stopping accuracy to her face. "I'm buying."

Just looking at his handsome face made her heart race. She didn't want to think about what it would be like to go on a date with him, never mind fantasize about what would happen at the end of the evening as they said good-night. Keeping her defenses up—and her thoughts at bay about being held against his tall strong body and kissed by those soft, sensual lips—she countered mildly, "I thought you didn't have any cash."

"I still have a credit card," he murmured with easy familiarity.

Ignoring his steady, probing gaze, she continued walking away from him. "Some cab companies take credit cards."

He waited until she swung around to face him again. "Then I'd miss our…date."

So this *was* a date. "It's ten-thirty on a Sunday night. Only the fast-food joints and the pancake houses are going to be open this late."

He shrugged his broad shoulders lazily. "Sounds fine to me. Let's go." He gestured for her to lead the way to her vehicle.

Cantankerously, Hannah stayed right where she was. "I haven't exactly agreed to go out with you yet."

"Buying you something to eat is the least I can do after interrupting your 'hustling' back there."

Hannah propped her hands on her waist, puzzled by the hint of derision in his low tone. "What is it you've got against me scrounging up a game of pool, anyway?" she inquired, refusing to be sidetracked by the dark woodsy scent of his aftershave. He had to know, from all the times she had played him and his brothers in Holly Springs, that she was bound to win.

Dylan raised his eyebrow. "Is that what you were doing?" he asked, his audacity unchecked.

As far as anyone else knew, yes it was. Although she couldn't quite ignore the hint of innuendo in Dylan's watchful gaze. "I wasn't trying to date the guy, Dylan," she explained dryly, continuing toward the minivan.

"Good, 'cause in case you didn't notice," Dylan continued, still observing her carefully as he fell into step beside her, "R. G. Yarborough is married."

Hannah wasn't surprised Dylan had noticed the wedding ring R. G. Yarborough had been wearing when she had approached him for a game, then ever so discreetly slipped into his pants pocket when he thought she wasn't looking. Dylan noticed everything. Especially, apparently, the sleazy elements of her would-have-been companion for the duration of the evening. Not that Hannah intended to discuss with Dylan why it had been so important she hook up with the rich son of a gun, anyway.

"So?" Hannah kept her focus on Dylan as she unlocked the repair-shop minivan and slid open the back passenger door so he could get his clothes. "Last time I heard, it wasn't against the law for married men to play pool."

Dylan unzipped the bag and drew out a pair of jeans, a knit polo shirt, sweat socks and running shoes. He tossed the bag aside, then prepared to climb into the back. "Mind if I change?"

Yes, as a matter of fact, she did. "Wait till we get where we're going to eat," Hannah said, pretending she hadn't been affected at all by his earlier quick-change artistry. "I've seen enough of your studly body for one day."

Dylan flashed a surprisingly wicked grin. "Turned you on, huh?" he said, tossing his clothes down and climbing into the front-passenger seat inside.

If you only knew, Hannah thought. She was still burning from the glimpses of his handsome body. "You wish." She threw the taunt over her shoulder as she circled around the front of the van and climbed behind the steering wheel.

Dylan relaxed in the passenger seat, looking debonair and sexy, and very much ready to take a woman to bed. Which was ridiculous given that generally speaking he didn't even know she was alive, let alone a woman. Although you wouldn't know it the way he kept glancing at the way her skirt was riding up over her thighs…

Shaking off the wistful transgression—the day she would get Dylan's attention in that way was never going to come!—Hannah started up the vehicle and eased away from the curb. "So where do you want to go?" she asked in the most casual voice she could manage, wishing he didn't still look and smell so good.

"There's a drive-in root-beer stand en route back to Holly Springs. What do you say we stop there? That is if they take credit cards." He looked worried.

"I think I can handle it even if they don't," Hannah said dryly. She might not be rolling in dough, but she made more than enough to handle her day-to-day expenses as well as anything she felt like doing after hours.

"If it's cash only, I'll pay you back tomorrow," Dylan said, giving her another curiously analytical look.

"No problem," Hannah said.

The silence strung out between them. "You don't look happy," Dylan said eventually.

Hannah released a long, irritated sigh. "Should I be?" Given that he had just interrupted a very important get-to-know-you session she had planned. Not that she could have continued her preplanned manipulation of events with Dylan standing there, watching every move she made, without revealing what she and Cal were trying to accomplish when it came to R. G. Yarborough.

"Are you disappointed that guy you were with tonight turned out to be married?"

Hannah blinked in surprise as Dylan favored her with a challenging half smile she found even more disturbing than his sudden interference in her life.

"You were flirting with him," Dylan said.

Just as a means to an end, Hannah admitted to herself. But Dylan didn't need to know about any of that. "He's a little old for me. Don't you think?"

"He still looked like he wanted to take you to bed."

Hannah's neck and shoulders drew tight as a bow. *Be blunt, why don't you?* "And that surprises you?" Hannah asked coolly, flushing despite herself.

"That someone would want to take you to bed?"

Hannah tingled all over at the low timbre of Dylan's voice. With effort Hannah kept her eyes on the road and her hands on the steering wheel. She was not going to let Dylan Hart lead her down that path! She was not! "R. G. Yarborough never said that."

Dylan smirked. "Trust me." Dylan lounged in his seat, radiating all the pure male power and sexy masculinity he typically did on the TV screen. He turned to look at her directly. "The way you were coming on to him, he would've gotten around to suggesting it before the end of the night," Dylan predicted darkly.

Hannah knew that was true. The moment she'd walked up to tell her mark why she was there, only to have him suggest the two of them play a game of pool instead, R. G. Yarborough had looked her over like a piece of meat. "And that bothers you?" Hannah asked, completely surprised that Dylan sounded almost…jealous.

Suddenly, it was Dylan's turn to hedge.

DYLAN WAS PUSHING TOO hard. He knew it. But the curiosity was eating him up inside. He had to know what was going on between Hannah and Cal. Because if it was what it looked like at first glance, Cal and Hannah were both in a heap of trouble. He couldn't let either of them crash and burn without trying to stop it. "You just don't seem the type to pick up men in a bar," Dylan explained finally.

Now he had really hit a sore spot with her. She was taking his observation as an assault on her morality, when that wasn't what he had meant at all.

"I hope you know you're buying me one of everything on the menu for that remark," she said as she turned the minivan into the restaurant parking lot and angled it into one of the slots on either side of the concrete divider. She rolled down the windows and warm August air poured over them.

A waitress on roller skates headed over to the car. She handed them a plastic-coated menu. She told them about the specials, then gave them a few moments to decide. As soon as the waitress skated off,

Dylan turned back to Hannah and picked up the conversation where they had left off. "I meant that in the most respectful way," he said, doing his best to repair the damage.

"Did you now." Hannah kept her eyes glued on the menu.

It was late, but the place was full of teenagers in cars. All of whom seemed to be having a very good time—unlike he and Hannah.

Oh, to go back to such easy, carefree days…

"I'm concerned about your well-being and safety," Dylan continued.

Hannah turned back to him. She was about to speak, when the phone clipped to Dylan's belt began to ring.

Frowning, Dylan picked it up. "Dylan Hart," he said as the waitress roller-skated past them, balancing a tray filled with food. While he listened to the voice on the other end of the connection, she attached it to the driver-side window on the station wagon beside him. The delicious aromas of onion rings and chili dogs with cheese wafted up around them.

"It happened," Sasha, the Chicago evening-news anchor, said. "Just like you said it was going to."

Dylan tensed as Hannah went back to studying her menu. "When?"

"Tonight around six," Sasha said grimly. "Check your e-mail. The official notification should be there."

Dylan clamped down on a string of swearwords. "Thanks."

"No problem. And Dylan…" Sasha paused, empathy in her low voice. "I'm sorry."

"Same to you," Dylan replied just as sympathetically. He hung up to find Hannah watching him. "Mind if we take a rain check on dinner?"

Her eyes widened. She couldn't believe his audacity. "First you interrupt my evening. Now you're standing me up?"

Sometimes life really bites. "I need to get back to Holly Springs."

Hannah paused, her indignation fading as fast as it had appeared. She looked at him harder. "Something wrong?"

"A problem with my job," Dylan muttered, reluctant to tell her anything more until he saw it in print and knew for certain his life was really crashing down around him.

Hannah hesitated, her lips taking on a softer curve. "Anything I can do?" she asked after a moment.

Dylan shrugged, his mood turning grimmer by the minute as he contemplated the days ahead. He was supposed to be in Holly Springs all week, on vacation. "I need to look at my e-mail as soon as possible. Do you have a computer with Internet access that I can use?"

Hannah continued to study him, knowing, as did

he, that every single member of his family had computers, at home and at work, yet he wasn't asking any of them. She had to be asking herself why. Yet, she didn't ask *him*.

"Sure." She shrugged her slender shoulders gracefully.

Dylan hadn't expected such kindness. He knew, after the way he had behaved toward her this afternoon and evening, that he certainly hadn't earned it. "That's it? That's all your questions?" He regarded her just as closely.

Hannah shrugged and signaled the waitress that they were finished with the menus. She shook her head in a way that let him know she had weathered her own share of personal crises. "The look on your face is answer enough."

DYLAN EXPECTED Hannah's Craftsman-style brownstone to look like every other eighty-year-old house in Holly Springs. Low ceilings, small cramped rooms, outdated everything. Instead, it looked like a demolition zone inside.

"What happened here?" he asked. He had been in her house a few times years ago, when he was a kid, recruiting Hannah for a game of pick-up baseball or soccer. A natural athlete, she had never failed to disappoint.

"When my grandfather died, I had a choice to either sell it or live in it. I decided if I was going to live in it I was going to make it my own. So for the past two years I've been remodeling, a little at a time."

"And then some." Dylan looked around. The original low ceilings had been completely ripped out, doing away with most of the attic and exposing the house's sloping fifteen-foot roofline. Three-quarters of the drywall had been redone, the rest was still waiting.

"I tore everything out and hired a contractor to put in new wiring and plumbing to bring it up to code. And built that—" Hannah pointed to the end of the house, away from what was going to be a central downstairs living area.

She led him toward the stairway. He followed her up. On the other side of the waist-high white beadboard wall that ran the length of the loft was a bedroom. Hannah had left the brownstone chimney exposed. A queen-size brass bed with a surprisingly frilly white lace comforter was pushed up against it. Her bridesmaid dress and the bouquet she had carried down the aisle were scattered across it. On one side of the room was a desk, with laptop computer and printer, the other side had a television and stereo. Beyond, he could see a pretty, white and ocean-blue bathroom, with private water closet, a pedestal sink, separate ceramic-tiled shower and clawfoot tub big enough for two. There was also a linen closet and an astonishing number of bath salts and scented lotions, makeup and shampoos. The windows were covered with pleated, ocean-blue-fabric blinds.

"As you can see, this is where I'm doing most of my living."

"Nice," Dylan said, meaning it. By putting in the loft, she had added another five hundred or so square feet to the thousand already downstairs.

"It will be when I finish," Hannah said, already booting up her computer while peering into a walk-in closet that seemed to contain mostly jeans, T-shirts and the one-piece coveralls she wore when working on cars down at the garage. "You know how to access your e-mail from someone else's computer?" Hannah asked as the home page—some car mechanic's site—came across the monitor.

Dylan nodded.

"I'll be downstairs. Yell if you need anything." She disappeared down the loft stairs.

"Thanks," Dylan said.

Unfortunately, the news was as bad as Sasha had predicted. Dylan had known it was coming. Still, he was stunned.

Knowing he'd want to read the letter from the TV station later, he printed a copy then shut the computer and printer off. Still feeling as if he had been kicked in the gut, he headed downstairs. Hannah was perched on a sawhorse in the middle of the gutted first floor, a small carton of premium ice cream in hand. She had a plastic spoon in her mouth as she surveyed the unfinished wide-plank floors and partially finished drywall. "I'm painting everything down here white, too," she told him. "And I'm going to leave the wood natural and protect it with polyurethane."

"What about your kitchen cabinets?" Dylan asked.

Hannah got up and walked over to the stainless-steel refrigerator. Aside from the microwave, it was the only appliance currently in the house. There wasn't even a kitchen sink, although there was a half bath with original basin nearby.

"They're white beadboard, similar in style to what I have upstairs in the master bath. I've got 'em in boxes, in the garage, along with the rest of the paint and the wallboard and the kitchen appliances— which I was lucky enough to get at cost a few months ago. Just haven't had the money to have any of it installed. Yet."

Was that what she had been doing at the pool hall? Trying to get together enough money to finish the inside of her home? It was a laudable goal, even if the means weren't to be commended.

She paused, her hand on the handle of the fridge. She studied him curiously. "Get what you needed up there?"

Dylan nodded.

"Then how come you still look like you just lost your best friend?"

Close, Dylan thought with a sad sigh. Then finding he needed someone to confide in—someone with a guy's gut sense when to stop with the questions—and a woman's compassionate heart, he said simply, "It was my job." He watched her carefully for reaction. "I got fired tonight."

Hannah took the news in stride, as he had hoped she would, and opened the freezer compartment. "Then you're going to be needing this," she said wryly as she took out another pint of ice cream and handed it to him, along with a plastic spoon.

There was no judgment in her eyes, only silent sympathy.

His hand warmed at the contact of her fingers brushing his. He looked down at the label, fighting the feeling of failure. Six years and four jobs in the business had taught him that television news was a brutal medium in which to work. "You think mocha cocoa crunch will help?"

"Ice cream always helps. So does chocolate." She reached over and touched his hand, more gently this time, before resuming her perch on the sawhorse. "I'm sorry about your job, Dylan."

"Me, too," he said honestly. He pried off the cardboard top of his ice cream. Although it had been irrational, he'd hoped to escape this bloodbath. Forcing himself to be a man about it, he looked into her eyes. "But that's the way it goes in my line of work. New owners mean new management, which means new staff." Usually in pretty quick order. Which was what had happened here.

She took another bite, then licked the back of the spoon. "Did you get severance pay?"

Telling himself to not even think about what her mouth would feel like under his, Dylan concentrated on answering her question. "Two months."

"Well that's good. Besides, a guy with your looks? You'll probably find something right away. Meantime—" Hannah waved her spoon for emphasis "—you've got the support of the entire Hart family."

Dylan let the rich chocolate slide down his throat and tried not to dwell on the fact this was the first time in his life he'd been fired—from anything. "I'm not telling them." He paused to let his words sink in. "Not until I have another job, anyway. And I'd appreciate it if you didn't, either."

If she was shocked she had the grace not to show it. "Whatever you want. Although that begs the question." She looked deep into his eyes. "If you're not telling them, why tell *me?*"

Why indeed? It wasn't like him to trust someone he knew he shouldn't trust. Not since he had been involved with Desirée, anyway. "'Cause I'm going to be needing access to a computer while I'm in town this week," he said calmly. "And I was hoping you'd let me use yours."

A teasing light crept into Hannah's emerald-green eyes as she gave him the slow, thoughtful once-over. "Do I get to charge you?"

Depends, Dylan thought. How badly do you need the money?

Hannah's phone rang. Her eyes still on his, she pulled the receiver off the kitchen wall. "Hannah. Yeah, hi. No, I didn't, sad to say. Because we got interrupted. Not to worry. I've at least got him interested. Yeah, ten to one he'll call. If I'm lucky, tomorrow or the next day. I promise. 'Night."

"Anyone I know?" Dylan asked, wondering if that had been Cal and how he felt about that if it had been.

"I make it a policy never to talk and tell. So…" She gestured around her. Dylan could see chalk outlines on the floors, where all the appliances, and the sink and so on were to go. "What do you think about what I've done so far with my downstairs?" she asked.

"I like it." Dylan studied the layout of the roughed-in kitchen that overlooked the backyard. "When will you be done?"

Hannah frowned. "I'm not really sure. Depends on the money situation. Materials aren't so bad. It's the labor that's so costly."

Dylan figured it would take thousands of dollars to finish what she had started. And although the upstairs was nice, the downstairs was barely livable. He couldn't imagine living like this for the two years she said it had been going on. No wonder she was getting antsy. "You can't get a second mortgage?" he asked helpfully.

"Already maxed out on that avenue. That's how I got all the materials and the upstairs done."

Dylan searched for alternatives. "What about doing the labor yourself?"

"I want it to look professional." Finished with her ice cream, Hannah put the lid back on and slid it into the freezer compartment. "Besides, it'll all get done eventually, as soon as I get my bank account built up."

Finding he had little appetite, Dylan handed over his ice-cream container, too. "You could always moonlight."

Hannah gave Dylan an even glance. But the confession he hoped to coax from her, about what she and his brother had been up to that evening, didn't come. "I suppose," she said eventually.

"Or you could ask your friends to help you out."

Hannah planted her hands on her hips. "Like who, for instance?" she asked drolly.

Dylan held her gaze, not sure why he was volunteering, just knowing he was. And not just for Cal's sake. "Like me."

Hannah's auburn eyebrow arched. "Are we friends?"

Good question. And one he intended to answer. "I

don't know." Dylan took her into his arms, cupped her chin in his hand and tilted her face up to his. "Let's see."

Chapter Three

The way Dylan had been looking at her since they'd met up at Sharkey's Pool Hall, Hannah could swear he knew what she was up to. And more—disapproved of her methods of getting his brother what Cal wanted and needed to turn his life around.

Not that Dylan could possibly know anything of the secret she was sharing with his doctor-brother, Hannah reassured herself bluntly as Dylan's lips came impossibly closer to hers.

"You're not going to kiss me," Hannah murmured as she splayed her hands across the hard, warm surface of his chest.

Dylan's sexy grin merely widened. "Want to bet?" he said.

And then his lips were on hers, and so many emotions poured through Hannah all at once. Shock that he dared to put the moves on her, amazement that she was actually letting him. She had never felt anything like the sweet seduction of Dylan Hart, never melted in anyone's arms this way. The depth of her response, the way she got caught up in the unhurried pressure of his lips, and the liquid stroking of his tongue shook her to her soul.

Furious at both him and herself—she didn't give this part of herself away to just anyone!—she clamped her lips together. To no avail. He subtly traced the seam and worked them apart using a mixture of pressure and temptation that was unlike anything Hannah had ever dreamed or felt. Pressing her even tighter against his hard, muscled length, he kissed her again and again as if there were no tomorrow for either of them. And as desire swirled inside her and caught flame, she could almost…almost…believe it. Probably would have, if the hard lessons of life hadn't taught her to protect her heart.

"Darn it all, Dylan," Hannah told him breathlessly when at last he lifted his head. "You had no business laying one on me—especially like that!" She felt herself flushing as he cupped her face between his hands.

"I still want to do it again," he whispered, looking down at her.

And so did she, Hannah thought on a beleaguered groan as she surged right back into his arms. Right or wrong, who cared, when it felt so darn good…

Dylan had started this on impulse. Mostly as a

test. To see if Hannah kissed like the experienced lady of the evening she had acted and sounded like back at the Wedding Inn, when she had been receiving instructions from Cal. Instead, the delectable Hannah Reid kissed as if she was all of sixteen, sweetly and awkwardly at first, tentativeness turning to enthusiasm, shy reserve to passion. And it was that mixture of innocence and ardor that was nearly his undoing. Because when their mouths were fused together like this, when he felt the responsiveness of her lips moving with sweet deliberation against his, it was all he could do to hold his own passion in check. It had been so long since he'd felt anything genuine or spent time with anyone this complicated and challenging. And he needed that, he was beginning to realize. Needed this…unbridled passion.

Unfortunately, because of the situation with his brother and his suspicions about Hannah, he couldn't give in to it. At least not yet.

Hearts pounding, regrets already forming—on both sides—they drew apart. Hannah looked at him as if she wanted to kiss him and smack him for his audacity simultaneously.

He knew how she felt. He wanted to kiss her and smack himself, too.

Then, as he sort of knew she would, she composed herself admirably. Becoming the cool, unflappable Hannah who hung out with the guys and never

ever let anything faze her, once again. "You really have to leave," she told him firmly, in responsible-grown-up mode again.

He found himself wishing the reckless teenager would come back. For just one more kiss. Maybe two?

"Now," Hannah continued, giving him an even look. "Before we do something we're both going to wish we hadn't."

Dylan nodded, knowing that was the shrewdest course. Now all he needed was a plausible excuse to stay close enough to her to be able to find out what she was up to with Cal. His being fired was it. "Can I come back in the morning? Hang out here during the day so I can make phone calls and do e-mails and start looking for another job?" After all, she wouldn't be here, she would be at her auto repair shop.

Hannah studied him as if wondering what he was up to. "Why not go back to Chicago if you want to do that?"

"There's too much tea and sympathy waiting for me there," Dylan told her truthfully. And frankly, he didn't want to hear it. "And it would raise my family's suspicions if I were to cut my visit short again and go back without warning." He'd done that the previous week and ended up missing Janey and Thad's wedding rehearsal and dinner. He was still in the doghouse with his mother over that one.

"And you're hanging out here at my place all day

long won't draw their curiosity?" Arms folded in front of her, Hannah regarded him skeptically.

Dylan shrugged, and moved his glance away from the soft, rounded curves of her breasts beneath the clinging tank top. "I'll tell them I volunteered to help you get a handle on your renovations," he temporized. "Help you finish some drywalling or painting or something."

She continued studying him astutely. "And why would you do that?"

"As penance for inconveniencing you so much this afternoon and almost making you late for Janey and Thad's wedding, too."

She didn't disagree that he owed her. "You've got all the angles covered, don't you?"

"For tomorrow, anyway. So, do we have a deal?"

"On one condition."

Dylan waited.

"No more kisses."

"Unless, of course, you initiate them." He grinned.

Hannah scoffed. "I wouldn't hold your breath waiting for *that* to happen."

Given the way she was looking at him now, he wouldn't either. Still, he owed her. "You're a real pal, Hannah," Dylan told her as they headed companionably for the door. "Not that it's any surprise you're so understanding," he continued, glad the mood was relaxing between them once again.

The shift from potential lover to platonic buddy was not as welcome as Dylan had hoped it would be to Hannah. "And why is that?" she asked him warily. She paused, her hand on the doorknob.

"I don't know exactly." Dylan struggled to put into words his feelings about her natural ability to put a man at ease. "Maybe because you've spent so much time with the guys, growing up, you're almost like one of us. And bottom line," he said as he patted her on the back in lieu of the kiss good-night he would have preferred, "guys help their buddies out."

"ONE OF THE GUYS," Hannah was still fuming the next morning when she went to work at the garage. Didn't that just take the cake!

"I don't think he was trying to insult you, honey," Slim Kerstetter said. Hannah's only employee, the sixty-year-old Slim had worked at the garage since he was a teenager himself, staying on after Hannah's grandfather died and the business came into her hands. "He was probably just trying to compliment you, and it came out all wrong. Guys do that, you know."

Hannah glanced at Slim. As usual, Slim was wearing baggy jeans and a short-sleeved shirt rolled up to expose his biceps. He'd been to the barber the day before and his salt-and-pepper hair was shorn down to a quarter-inch. "Not in this case," Hannah said. "In this instance, Dylan Hart knew exactly what he was saying."

Slim sent her a sly look. The fact he was a life-long bachelor with only one real love—NASCAR—did not keep him from dispensing romantic advice. "If you want him to see you as a girlie-girl, start dressing and acting like one." Slim removed the fuel pump from the Lexus he was working on while Hannah continued running diagnostics on a Mercedes.

"If I did that, no one would want me working on their cars," she said.

"Then you got yourself a dilemma, don't you, sweetheart?" Slim teased as a familiar Lamborghini pulled in.

"Hey, Hannah," Emma Donovan-Hart waved at Hannah cheerfully as she got out of the car. "I brought my dad's car in for servicing."

"That was nice of you," Hannah said to her good friend, who was the premiere wedding planner in the area. She wished she could feel even one tenth as bliss-fully in love and contented as Emma looked these days.

Emma strode closer, her cap of dark, chin-length curls bouncing as she moved. "Yeah, well, Dad's having a crisis with the hockey team. Seems one of the Carolina Storm's announcers quit yesterday to take a job with the Cable Sports News network. He's getting his own weekly interview show, so it's a great opportunity for him. My parents both wish him well, but now they're in a mess because they need to hire his replacement by week's end."

"Do you need a ride to work at the Wedding Inn?"

"Thanks, but Joe's taking me over."

No sooner had Joe and Emma driven off than Cal Hart pulled in. "You want to get that or shall I?" Slim said.

"I'll handle it," Hannah said, walking out to Cal. The six-foot-two surgeon had ash-blond hair and gray eyes and an easygoing, compassionate nature Hannah warmed to. Whereas Dylan was her age—Cal was thirty-four. Because Cal had been so far ahead of her in school, she hadn't known him all that well until two years ago when he returned to Holly Springs to practice medicine. Now he was like a brother to her.

"Let's go up to my office," Hannah said. "It's more private there." She led the way through the garage, up the stairs at the back, down a short hall, past the garage's only bathroom, to a small room that overlooked the alley. It was crowded with file and supply cabinets, two chairs, a desk, phone and the computer she used for looking up parts and obscure repair manuals on the Internet. These days, a computer and all the information that could be gleaned from one was a mechanic's best tool.

"Sorry I phoned so late last night," Cal said.

Hannah knew how upset Cal had been lately. Her heart went out to him. It was rough, not knowing where you stood, or if and when things would ever work out. "No problem."

"I got the feeling I was interrupting something," Cal said.

No kidding, Hannah thought, her mind going back to the fevered kisses that had left her reeling, both physically and emotionally. "Your brother Dylan was there." Briefly, Hannah explained how Dylan had tracked her down to get his suitcase.

Cal sighed and shoved his hands through the short, traditionally cut layers of his hair. "So you didn't even have time to shoot a game of pool with R. G. Yarborough," he noted, obviously disappointed.

About that, Hannah felt only relief. "No, but I had plenty of time to size him up," she told Cal grimly. "Yarborough's every bit as narcissistic and self-centered as you said. To get what we want from him we're going to have proceed carefully."

SLIM KERSTETTER GRINNED as Dylan walked up. "Beginning to look like a regular Hart family reunion around here," he drawled as he moved a car up in the air via hydraulic lift.

"Say again?" Dylan blinked.

"First Emma and Joe." Slim picked up his tools and stepped beneath the belly of the vehicle. "Then Cal. Now you. And not a one of you had an appointment to get your car fixed. Yep. I'd say that's a record, all right."

And Cal's Jeep was still parked in one of the

spaces. Dylan pushed away the feeling of unease. "Where is Hannah?" he asked.

"In her office." Slim pulled a kerchief from his pocket and mopped the sweat from his forehead. "And Dylan—a word to the wise. You plan to get anywhere with that gal, you got to stop treating her like one of the guys."

What the hell was that about? Hannah couldn't have told him about the kisses they'd shared, or had she? "I'll take that under advisement." Pulse picking up, Dylan rounded the corner, past the hydraulic lifts, to the stairs at the rear of the garage.

He mounted them silently and strode just as soundlessly down the short hall, beyond the restroom. The door to her office was closed. Through the glass top half he could see Hannah sitting on the desk, her face tilted up at Cal. They were talking intently. Or so it appeared. As Dylan neared, their voices drifted toward him. "Difficult but not impossible," Hannah was saying. "Trust me. If there's anything I know, it's men and their—"

"Well, yeah," Cal concurred, his voice cutting off whatever it was she'd said.

"Everyone has a weakness," Hannah continued matter-of-factly. "Something in his life that'll make him prone to deal. We just have to find his. And as soon as we do—"

"I feel kind of sleazy just talking about this," Cal lamented, running both hands through his hair.

Jealousy twisted Dylan's gut as he watched Hannah reach over and pat Cal's arm.

"I wouldn't lose any sleep over our…" She hesitated, as if searching for the proper word.

"Manipulation?" Cal guessed dryly.

Hannah dropped her hand. "What is important is that we get what you want and come out ahead," Hannah continued sternly.

"It still feels like a con job," Cal protested in a low, guilty voice.

Hannah shrugged her slender shoulders. "So what if it is? You've got to think about the end result here, Cal, and what you stand to gain. Forget about R. G. Yarborough's feelings and well-being. I guarantee he isn't giving a thought to either yours or mine."

So what was this? Dylan wondered, stepping back out of sight of the office door and into the restroom. Some type of con job? Last night he'd thought it was Cal pushing Hannah to do something she didn't want to do. This morning it sounded as if it was the other way around.

The office door opened. Cal walked out briskly and headed right down the hall. Dylan waited until his brother had disappeared from view then stepped around the corner and into the office. Hannah was in the process of booting up her computer. Her cheeks flushed a pretty pink when she saw him, but that could have been as much from the memory of the kisses they'd shared the evening before as anything. Certainly, she didn't look as though she knew he had been spying on her.

"What brings you here?" she asked.

Easy, he thought, glad for the excuse. "Your house key."

DYLAN WAS DOING IT AGAIN, looking at her almost suspiciously, as if he knew what she was up to with his brother. But that was impossible. No one but she and Cal knew about the transaction they were trying so hard to pull off.

"Oh yeah." Hannah fished the spare out of her desk and handed it to him. "Don't lose it."

"I won't," Dylan promised.

Their hands brushed. Their gazes meshed. And in that instant, Hannah knew Dylan had slept lightly, if at all, the previous night. Not that she could blame him. Losing your job, especially when your work meant as much to you as Dylan's did to him, had to be devastating. She would have lain awake all night, staring at the ceiling, too. Wanting to help him, she said, "You ever thought about announcing instead of sportscasting?"

Dylan made a face. "Different talent."

"Yes, but if you had the chance, would you do it?" Hannah persisted.

He shrugged his broad shoulders amiably. "Sure."

"What do you know that I don't?" he asked, studying her face.

Delighted to be able to deliver some good news, she said, "One of the Storm's announcers just quit. They're filling the position by week's end."

HANNAH WENT HOME PROMPTLY at six that evening. Dylan wasn't there. Nor was there any note for her, or any way of knowing if he would even be back that evening. No painting or drywalling had been done, but there was plenty of evidence of his job search in the neat stacks of paper all over her bed.

Feeling glum, she had rushed to get home to see how his day had gone to no avail, Hannah dropped her grimy clothes in the hamper and stepped into the shower to scrub off the day. Mindful of the steamy August heat, she put on a dark green V-necked T-shirt and denim shorts, and was still combing out the tangles in her hair when she heard the front door open and close.

She walked down the stairs from the loft just as Dylan walked in to the open downstairs area. He was wearing the same suit and tie he'd had on the previous day at the airport. One hand held two large carry-out sacks from the root-beer stand they had been at the evening before; in the other was a cardboard carrying tray containing two large drinks.

"What's all this?" Hannah asked as the delicious aroma of chili, cheese and onion rings filled the air.

"The rain check on the dinner I owe you—one of everything on the menu plus some extra chili dogs with cheese and onion in case you're still as wild about them as I am. Are you?"

Hannah nodded. There was nothing like it, in her estimation, as far as junk food went. Funny he would think so, too, when in every other way they were so different. Usually guys wanted to buy her very hip or gourmet food—when they even asked her—and that was usually as payment for taking a look under the hood of their car or diagnosing a particularly perplexing electrical or mechanical problem with their vehicle. Nobody ever just bought her dinner for the sake of it, or went out of their way to spend time with her, one on one. Which begged the question. Why was Dylan suddenly so eager to spend time with her? Why was he suddenly hanging around, when he could just as easily have avoided her, the way he had at Janey's wedding reception?

Was it because he wanted to continue to use her house as a temporary office while she was at work? Or was there something more going on here? Something that had to do with those series of kisses last night?

Dylan tilted his head at her, as if wondering what was on her mind. "I hope you haven't eaten," he said.

As if on cue, Hannah's stomach growled. "Ah, no, I haven't," she said, embarrassed.

"Good." He looked around them with a bemused

grin. "Although where we're going to eat is a good question. Where is your furniture?"

"I sold everything in a tag sale, to make more money to spend on the interior. I figure when it's all done, I'll just buy some new stuff that will fit the space."

"Makes sense. In the meantime, where do you usually eat?"

"Perched on one of the sawhorses. Or upstairs, on my bed," Hannah continued. "Sort of depends on what I'm eating."

He nodded at her, considering. "So where are we going to do this?"

It was so hot outside. The mosquitoes were fierce this time of year. "My bedroom, I guess," Hannah allowed finally. "You can sit at my desk. I'll sit on the floor."

He arched his eyebrow. "Not the bed?"

Hannah smiled wryly. "Somehow, eating chili dogs on a white bedspread doesn't seem like a good idea. And speaking of chili dogs." She narrowed her eyes at him. "Are you really going to eat this dressed in a suit?"

Dylan shrugged, unperturbed. "Unless you want me to strip down to my skivvies again."

"Uh, no," Hannah said hastily. She held up a hand in stop-sign fashion. "Once was enough."

He grinned again, in an appreciative male way

that made Hannah think he was considering making love to her then and there. Which was silly. Except for the kisses the night before, there had never been anything between them. And since he was leaving at the end of the week, off to Chicago or parts unknown again, there never would be. Unless...

"So. How's the job search going?" Hannah asked after they made their way upstairs to her bedroom. She settled picnic style on the rug in front of her walk-in closet and was surprised when Dylan by-passed the chair she had offered him and sat cross-legged opposite her. "Did you check out the announcing job for the Carolina Storm hockey team?"

Dylan took off his jacket and tie and tossed them onto her bed. "That's where I was this afternoon. I went over and auditioned."

Hannah watched as he undid the first few buttons on his shirt and rolled up his cuffs. "Already?"

He nodded, looking a lot more relaxed as he leaned against the wall and they divvied up the food. "Yeah. They were already vetting résumés and doing preliminary interviews, and anyone who passed muster was then eligible to get in line and go into a taping room. Basically, they handed us roster lists for both teams on the tape, as well as specific information they wanted worked into the broadcast. We all 'called'—or announced—the first twenty-minute period. Then we were taken into another room to video-tape a mock interview with one of the public relations staff, who was pretending to be either a player or a coach, and that was it. They're going to review all the applicants by week's end and have a decision no later than Monday."

Hannah tried not to notice how handsome Dylan looked in the soft, dusky light of her bedroom. "And being family to one of the current Storm players—"

"Will neither help nor hurt me." Seeming to read her mind, he got up and turned on a lamp. "It's all going to be decided on the basis of the tapes. Who-ever does the best job will get the position. Period."

Hannah unwrapped a chili dog. "Well, that's good."

Dylan sighed and sent her another imposing glance. "Yeah."

Hannah moved her glance from the exposed col-umn of his throat. "You don't look happy." She did not need to be wondering if the suntanned skin vis-ible in the open V of his shirt was as smooth as it looked, the springy light brown hair as crisp.

"Ah, you know how it is when you do something like this," Dylan answered casually, oblivious to the ardent direction of her thoughts. "At the time you're doing it, you think it's fine. Even great. Then as time goes on you start second-guessing yourself, wonder-ing if you should have said or done this or that."

Hannah did know. She just wouldn't have assumed someone as spectacularly pulled together as Dylan would have. "I always thought you were so confident," she said.

"I am."

"But?"

A mixture of sadness and despair crept into his eyes. "I guess I just want this job. I didn't realize how much until I went into the press box and began calling the game." His lips took on a determined slant. "It'd be so great to travel with the team and be part of the action, instead of just reporting the scores on the evening news."

He made what he did sound unimportant. It wasn't. "But you do interviews, too," Hannah protested.

Again, Dylan looked unimpressed. "In one- and two-minute spots from a prepared, vetted list of questions. It's not really the same as thinking on your feet."

He had a point there. Announcing a game as it was actually played had to be a lot harder. "Well, maybe you'll get the job," she said.

"Maybe… In the meantime, I've got half a dozen other leads to follow up."

"Ah, yes." Hannah grinned. "The papers on my bed."

Dylan smiled. "Sorry about that. I figured I'd be back to clean up the mess before you got home from work."

"That's okay." Although she liked to keep the only

finished area in her home looking good, she really was not high-maintenance in that regard. "What else is in the works?"

Briefly, he filled her in on the other jobs available.

"So it's Houston, San Francisco, Seattle, Cleveland, or here, basically," Hannah summed up, thinking how far away those places were, how little she would see Dylan if he got a job in any city other than Raleigh, North Carolina. Not that it should matter to her....

"Unless something else comes up. Which it well may. I called my sports and entertainment attorney, Ross Dempsey, this morning. He said he would put the word out that I was available to all his contacts in the business, so something may come up that way, too."

"Well, you've got time," Hannah encouraged. "Two months—"

"Technically, yeah." Dylan polished off a serving of onion rings, then crumpled up the paper bag. "But I don't want to not be working. It's too hard just sitting around doing nothing."

Hannah could imagine that was so. "Did you tell your family yet?" She searched his face.

"No. And I'm not going to, either," he said, his voice full of that stubborn Hart pride she knew so well.

"I learned a long time ago that keeping my worries to myself was the best way to proceed," Dylan continued firmly.

Aware they were headed into intimate territory, Hannah asked cautiously, "What do you mean?"

Dylan's bedroom eyes met and held hers again. "I was eight when my dad died," he told her quietly. "And all I wanted to do was crawl under the covers and cry."

Hannah had never had to deal with that kind of grief when her own parents passed away, as she had been just an infant, and far too little to know what was going on. "But you didn't," Hannah guessed.

Dylan's voice deepened compassionately and he continued in a calm, deliberate voice. "I couldn't, not when my mother was so devastated." He shook his head, recalling. "She had always been so strong and in charge. Then, suddenly, she was so fragile. Just figuring out what to have for dinner seemed beyond her."

Hannah could only imagine how terrifying that must have been for Helen's brood of six children, who, if memory served, had ranged in age from six to fifteen at the time.

Dylan paused as if to reharness his emotions. "I'm not sure what would have happened to us if my oldest brother, Mac, hadn't stepped in and taken charge of the family. He was only fifteen at the time, but he divided up all the chores and impressed upon us the need to hold things together for Mom, to keep a stiff upper lip, until she was able to pull herself together again. And it's a lesson that has served me well,"

Dylan continued, jaw set. "Because it didn't take me long to figure out if you could look like you were doing okay on the outside, chances were you were doing okay on the inside, too."

Hannah agreed, to a point. She wasn't sure, however, that the two situations commanded similar coping strategies. Especially when Dylan's family had the potential to be so helpful to him now. But how to convince him of that, she didn't know.

Downstairs, the doorbell rang.

Dylan looked over at her. "Expecting anyone?" he asked.

Chapter Four

"Oh my gosh!" Hannah said.

"Surprised I tracked you down?" R .G. Yarborough asked her as Hannah stepped out onto her front porch. Dylan was right beside her.

Hannah cast a hesitant look at Dylan before turning back to Mr. Midlife Crisis in Action. This evening he was wearing a body-hugging silver silk T-shirt, skintight black jeans, custom alligator boots and an onyx and diamond earring. And, of course, Dylan noted immediately, no wedding ring.

"Not really," Hannah countered, backing smoothly but efficiently away from the overpowering aroma of expensive cologne. She smiled at her drop-in visitor as if she didn't realize he was on the make. "I'm in the book, and I told you where I lived."

The married fifty-something smiled at Hannah. "I thought you might like to see my Mustang."

Dylan looked at the '64 convertible parked at the

curb. Bodywise, anyway, the cherry-red sports car looked to be in pretty good shape. And, he supposed, the vintage auto was one unthreatening way to get a classic-car mechanic like Hannah's attention. What Yarborough didn't know, of course, was that Hannah—and his brother—wanted something from Yarborough, too. What precisely, Dylan had yet to figure out. But he would, he reassured himself firmly. And he'd do it sooner rather than later, whether the too-clever-for-her-own-good Hannah Reid realized it or not.

"Maybe we could even go for a spin with the top down?" R.G. continued enthusiastically, looking at Hannah's damp auburn mane. "It'd be a great way to dry your hair. That is, if you don't mind the wind in your face."

Dylan expected Hannah to refuse. After all, she had company. Him. Instead, she smiled and said, "Just let me get my shoes and I'll be ready to go."

R.G. regarded Dylan complacently, as if he had just won the girl.

Dylan knew the contest—if indeed there was one—hadn't even begun.

"Okay. I'm ready!" Hannah breezed back out the front door. "Sorry, Dylan." She glanced at him apologetically.

"Oh, I don't mind," Dylan said as he stuck his hands in the pockets of his suit pants and followed them down to the curb. R.G. was already reaching in, letting down the top.

R.G. and Hannah looked at him curiously. "I'll just tag along," Dylan said, and before anyone could stop him, he stepped over and into the back seat.

"Want to drive?" R.G. tossed the keys at Hannah.

She caught them one-handed. "Love to!" Hannah enthused.

She climbed behind the wheel. R.G. took the front-passenger seat. Dylan took up the middle of the back seat. And they were off. Going, to Dylan's frustration—or was it satisfaction—no more than forty-five miles an hour, no matter how Hannah floored it. And she did…floor…it.

"Well," Hannah said when they returned to her house a good fifteen minutes later, and she had her nose stuck under the hood, right alongside R.G. "It's a pokey little thing, isn't it?"

Dylan lifted an eyebrow, surprised at the outright insult.

"Well, it's a '64 model," R.G. huffed.

Hannah remained visibly quite unimpressed. "I know a few guys who have '64s that will go eighty-five or ninety on the track."

R.G. scowled. His surgically tightened face began to redden. "I could have this souped up."

Hannah shook her head at R.G. as if the mere idea of that was ridiculous, then looked at Dylan and patted him on the arm. "Would you excuse us, hon? R.G. and I want a moment alone."

DYLAN WAS STILL FUMING when Hannah patted R. G. Yarborough on the arm and kissed him on the cheek, saying goodbye in casual southern style, then walked back in the house some half hour later.

Dylan knew the brush of Hannah's lips on the odious man's cheek had meant nothing. And, had it been anyone else but that vermin, the gesture wouldn't have registered as anything more than politeness. But it was Yarborough, and he was on the prowl for some action while his wife and kids were out of town. And Hannah, damn it, should have known better than to encourage the scum in any way.

And probably would have if she and Cal hadn't been cooking up some scheme of their own.

"You could have gone home, you know," Hannah observed as she joined him in the loft. He was seated in front of her computer again, busily answering e-mail.

Dylan's eyebrow lifted but his gaze remained fastened steadfastly on the screen in front of him. He told himself what he had been repeating for the last half hour. He was not feeling possessive toward Hannah in that distinctly "man and his woman" kind of way. Only suspicious.

"To Chicago?" Dylan played dumb on purpose.

"No," Hannah said dryly. She sat down on the corner of the desk, so she was facing him. She stretched her long, smooth legs out in front of her. "Your mother's place. Right next to The Wedding Inn. Remember?"

Dylan tried not to think about her sexy hyacinth perfume, or wonder just where on her slender body she had splashed it. "I'm not staying there this time." Finished with what he was doing, he shut down her laptop and closed the lid. Then stood. "The house is still full of relatives in town for Janey's wedding last weekend. I'm staying with Mac."

Dylan picked up his tie and suit coat from her bed.

"Then you could have gone to his place." She moved gracefully to let him pass.

"No—" Dylan consulted his watch as he headed down the loft stairs "—I couldn't."

This time it was Hannah on his heels. "And why, pray tell, is that?" She took the stairs every bit as speedily as he did.

Dylan looked around for someplace suitable to hang his jacket and finally draped it over one of the sawhorses, out of harm's way. "Because I needed to wait around for the drywall and paint and cabinet guys. They're all supposed to be here at eight."

Hannah blinked and skidded to a halt right in front of him. "What for?"

Dylan shrugged. The answer to that was obvious. "So you can show them what you want them to do."

Color swept into her face. "I can't pay for that," Hannah exclaimed.

Dylan caught her arms, which were flailing temperamentally, and forced them down. "You don't have to," he told her calmly. He arrowed a thumb at his chest. "I'm compensating them."

Looking even more beautiful in the dwindling daylight, Hannah narrowed her eyes at him suspiciously. "Compensating them how?" She leaned in even closer.

"With free tickets. I may have been fired, but I've already received complimentary season tickets to the Bulls and the Bears and the Blackhawks for next season. Not to mention all the pertinent college teams in the area. I'm probably not going to be in Chicago to use them, so I'm bartering them, on your behalf."

"Why would you do this for me?" Hannah asked, appearing stunned by the generosity of Dylan's gift.

Because he didn't want to owe her, and he did want her to have her home finished professionally. Because he didn't want her—and by extension his very married brother Cal—to have to do anything she and or Cal shouldn't be doing to get the money to finish her house renovation. Because he didn't want R. G. Yarborough flashing a bunch of cash or even vintage automobiles around and trying to make Hannah his lover.

But knowing he couldn't tell her all that, without

also letting on that he was on to the fact she was up to something, Dylan said simply, "I am doing this because you went out of your way and picked me up at the airport on Sunday and you're letting me camp out here and use your house and your computer all week."

Hannah went very still. "It's not exactly an even exchange."

"So?" Dylan sat down on the sawhorse and stretched his legs out in front of him. "You'll do something nice for me at some time in the future."

"Oh, no," Hannah declared suddenly, putting up both her hands in the age-old signal to back off. "No way am I doing *that* for you!" she said heatedly.

Dylan blinked. "Doing what?" he demanded, confused.

"Sleeping with you!" She leveled an accusing finger his way. "All week!"

"How about just one night then?" Dylan drawled, amused Hannah would jump to such an erroneous conclusion.

Like he had ever had to pay or barter for sex!

But then, given what Cal had appeared to be asking Hannah to do for him… Maybe this wasn't as rare an occasion as he would have normally thought. After all, Cal's wife had been in Honolulu for nearly two years now, with only infrequent visits back to the mainland. R. G. Yarborough's wife was currently away on vacation…. Was Hannah—who still reportedly had a hard time getting dates herself, mostly because of her tomboy antics as well as the nature of her profession—now easing her own lone-liness by keeping company with lonely men? Was she not interested in marriage per se, and merely looking to be someone's lover? The idea of having someone in your life just for sex had never appealed to Dylan, but he knew plenty of men who were into that, and he had found out the hard way there were women who felt the same. As for Hannah, well, he wasn't sure yet how she felt about sex. Did she want it to be as romantic as she deserved it to be? Was she so inexperienced she didn't know the difference between having sex with someone and making love? The only thing Dylan knew for certain was that Hannah had to be lonely in the same way he was these days, if she didn't have a significant other in her life.

"What's gotten into you?" Hannah demanded.

Dylan couldn't say. He only knew Hannah was getting to him in a way no woman ever had, prompt-ing him to think of her and her well-being ahead of even himself.

"Since when do you put the moves on me?" Han-nah continued, looking all the more ticked off. "We've never even had a date!"

At least that was a problem that was easily remedied,

Dylan thought. "I've got two tickets to the Children's Hospital benefit tomorrow evening. Go with me."

WHEN DYLAN ARRIVED to pick Hannah up at seven the following night, she was fresh out of the shower and clad in the usual post-work shorts and T-shirt.

"You're not ready," Dylan told her, looking both surprised and disappointed.

That's because she'd had time to come to her senses. It was one thing to be compassionate and offer an old friend a helping hand when he was fresh out of a job. Quite another to date him, even temporarily. Hannah smiled apologetically and lifted her shoulders in a helpless little shrug she had seen other women use to excellent result. "I've changed my mind. I'm not going."

For a moment, Dylan didn't react. "A little late to be canceling, don't you think?" he chided as he cast a look at the drywall, which had been completed while Hannah was at work that day. No doubt about it—the guy Dylan had bartered with had done a fantastic job. Real progress had been made.

Hannah shrugged again and found the completely feminine gesture completely ineffective this time. She smiled again, wondering just how people got themselves out of social engagements they never should have accepted in the first place. "I don't have anything to wear."

"Mmm, hmm." Dylan's glance covered her from the top of her damp head to her polished black-cherry toenails.

Despite her earlier determination to remain immune to his sexy imposing presence, Hannah heated everywhere his glance had covered.

"What's this?" He strode past her to the garment bag she'd left draped over a sawhorse, along with her shoulder bag. Dylan unzipped it and peered inside at the delicate fabric. "Looks perfect to me."

Exactly what Emma Donovan-Hart had said when Hannah borrowed the dress from her earlier in the day. Hannah ran her fingers through the damp auburn waves brushing across her face. She tucked a strand behind her ear. "I'm just not comfortable at big social affairs."

Dylan lifted an eyebrow in disbelief. "Have you ever been to one?"

Hannah pretended to misunderstand the question. "As a chauffeur?"

He regarded her in exasperation. "As a guest."

"Well, no—"

"That settles it, then." His low voice cut across her authoritatively. He took her hand and half led, half pushed her toward the loft. "You're going." He grabbed her garment bag en route. "If I have to haul you over my shoulder and carry you in there myself."

Hannah paused at the entrance to her bedroom. "You wouldn't!"

"Just watch me." Dylan paused, his expression gentling. "Come on, Hannah," he coaxed softly. "I guarantee you'll have a good time. If you don't, we'll leave. I just need to make an appearance because I promised I would. Then, if you want, we'll go elsewhere."

Hannah studied him. There was no doubt he wanted her to go with him. "You mean it?"

Dylan held up two fingers in the age-old pledge. "Scout's honor."

Hannah had to admit a date with Dylan was worth the pain of being a blue-collar girl in a white-collar world. It took fifteen minutes to dry her hair, spritz on some perfume, get into the dress and heels and apply a little evening makeup. The effort was well worth it, judging by the approving look on Dylan's face. "Now, that's amazing," he said, appreciating the completeness of her transformation. "Turn around so I can see the rest of you."

He was making her feel like Cinderella going to the ball. "Dylan—"

He motioned with his fingers.

Aware he wouldn't be satisfied until he had seen the rest of the dress, she pirouetted, blushing all the while. His eyes roved the shimmering gold sheath dress with the crocheted overlay. Hannah had thought the tank top-style bodice was a little low, but Emma had assured her it was just right. A thick gold choker, dangly earrings, wide gold bracelets and thin gold evening sandals completed the ensemble.

All the admiration she had ever wanted to see was in his eyes. "You look incredibly lovely." He lifted her hand and kissed the back of it.

For the first time in her life Hannah had an inkling of what it would be like to be "courted" and "pursued" instead of just "hung out with." There was a world of difference in the two approaches and the way they made her feel. Afraid she really could get used to this if she gave herself half a chance, Hannah murmured self-consciously, "Thank you."

Dylan slid his hand beneath her elbow as they walked to the car, leaving no doubt in her mind that this really was a date, instead of just two people going to the same event in the same vehicle. "You're going to be the prettiest woman there tonight," he continued with a mesmerizing smile.

"I don't know about that," Hannah said, chiding herself for getting so worked up about something that might not mean all that much to Dylan in the end. But there was no doubt her pulse was racing, her spirits revving into high gear, being with him like this. And Dylan was right as it turned out, Hannah discovered some thirty minutes later. To her relief, she was at least on par with everyone else in the well-heeled crowd, dresswise.

The benefit was being held on the Horton Fieldler Estate. Located just outside Durham, the gray stone château had been built in the early 1900s by the famed financier. Used for years as a summer place for the New York-based family, the luxurious three-story fifty-room mansion and well-landscaped grounds had eventually been opened for tours during the day, and rented out for parties in the evenings. Tonight's theme was the Arabian Nights, and the waitstaff were all dressed as characters from the classic tale. White silk tents spilled over the lawn. An orchestra played. There were at least a thousand people in attendance, Hannah realized as she and Dylan walked through security. Including, she spotted right off, the governor and prominent members of the legislature, locally based athletes and television personalities, and members of the Children's Hospital staff, all of whom were identified by special tags.

"Glad you could make it!" A stocky man with a dark brown goatee, bushy eyebrows and a wide infectious smile rushed up to them. He had a good ol' southern boy demeanor that had Hannah feeling immediately at ease.

Dylan smiled. "Hannah, this is Ted LaSalle, the station manager at W-MOL, my old boss."

"Mind if we go over here, where we can talk quietly for a moment?" Ted said.

Dylan looked at Hannah. She shrugged her okay, thinking he meant to leave her to fend for herself. Instead, the next thing she knew, Dylan had her elbow and she was moving with the two men to a quiet place in the trees.

"No use beating around the bush," Ted told Dylan as soon as they were out of earshot of others. "You're out of a job, and W-MOL would like nothing better than to have you back. So what do you say I have my secretary call you tomorrow and we set up a lunch date later in the week to discuss the possibility of your returning to the Raleigh station where your career began?"

Dylan smiled. "That sounds great, Ted."

"All right." Ted slapped him on the back. "I'll talk to you later. Meantime, have a good time, both of you."

"We will," Dylan promised, looking as polished and together as ever in a sophisticated sage-green summer suit, paler shirt and tie. "And thanks again for the tickets."

"No problem." Ted winked and was off.

Hannah looked up at Dylan, knowing now why it had been so important to him that he attend, why he'd been so concerned when she hadn't been ready on time. She'd thought it was because he wanted to go out with her on a real dress-up date, that this was perhaps the start of some new phase—however short-lived—in their lives. "So that's all this was?" she asked in a cheerful voice meant to disguise the disappointment she felt deep inside. She searched his face. "A preliminary job interview?"

"Not to mention a chance to see you in a dress again." He winked at her and said in a soft, low voice that sent thrills coursing over her skin, "And a very sexy one at that."

Hannah's glance drifted to the playful curve of his lips, the seductive glint in his eyes, then immediately moved away. "I'm serious, Dylan."

"Okay." Dylan considered her for a moment, then leaned closer, bringing with him the tantalizing scent of his cologne and the clean-soap-and-shampoo scent of his hair and skin. "Seriously, Ted LaSalle telephoned me yesterday afternoon and said he had a couple extra tickets to tonight's gala, would I consider going and bringing a date. I knew what it was probably leading up to, so I said yes."

Hannah's shoulders stiffened. Her back ramrod straight, she moved away from him. "And since I'm the only one of your gal-friends who knows you were fired, you had to ask me."

"No." Dylan moved closer and waited until he was assured of her attention before he continued. "Since you're the only one I wanted to come with me tonight, I had to ask you."

Their eyes held as Hannah bit into her lower lip and struggled to understand the significance of that. Was Dylan trying to tell her he was interested in her as a woman? All she knew for sure was that he was looking as if he wanted to kiss her again, and he couldn't kiss her, not in such a public place. She swallowed hard, trying not to let her hopes rise too much, unless something much more substantial than a fling was possible between them. Because she could really get her heart broken here. "Are you serious about taking a job in North Carolina?" she asked softly. Because if he was...

"I don't know." Dylan frowned, looking suddenly all business again. "The Raleigh market—in terms of money and viewership—is much smaller than Chicago. Taking a job at W-MOL again would sort of feel like going backward in my career and I'm not sure I want to do that."

Hannah understood, even as she struggled with her disappointment as she realized Dylan was indeed going to be leaving Holly Springs again, probably sooner rather than later.

"But since I got my start there, I at least want to hear what Ted LaSalle has to offer me," Dylan said "It's possible we could work out something on a temporary basis, since finding a comparable position in a place I want to live could take some time."

So if he did accept a job here again, it probably wouldn't be for long, Hannah concluded unhappily. And since her business was here, where did that leave them?

"HANNAH? Is that—? My God, it *is* you!"

On her way back from the powder room, Hannah froze at the sound of the familiar voice. Oh, no. Of all the times she did not need to run into her ex-boyfriend...

"Wow!" Rupert Wallace said, looking her up and down.

Across the room, Dylan continued to do what he had been doing most of the evening—hold court with a throng of starstruck admirers while Hannah chatted it up with one well-heeled Classic Car Auto Repair customer after another. All of whom, sad to say, had been equally stunned to see Hannah here. Apparently, they couldn't imagine her doing anything but working on an engine, either.

Rupert strolled uncomfortably close. An inch shorter than Hannah when she wasn't wearing heels, her ex was as fit and trim as ever. He was dressed in an expensive Italian suit and silk T-shirt. He had an artificially perfect tan and his dark curly hair had been shorn and gelled in a way that made him look all the more sophisticated. Hannah couldn't be sure, but it looked as if he'd had a nose job since she had seen him last.

"I can't believe how well you clean up." Rupert let out a low whistle and shook his head. "If I'd have known you could look like that—!"

"You would have what?" Hannah couldn't help

but cut in acerbically. "Married me, instead of that year's Miss North Carolina?"

Rupert had the grace to look chagrined. "Well, now, I wouldn't go that far," he drawled, as if he had nothing to be sorry for.

"I didn't think you would," Hannah said grimly, not sure why this still bothered her so much, except that she hated to be made the fool.

Rupert clamped a friendly hand on her shoulder, acting as if he hadn't run around with another woman behind her back. "Amber and I—well, we were meant to be. But that doesn't mean I haven't missed you tons since we split up," he continued in a low, oily voice. "Besides, you know the two of us were never meant to be serious…"

Then what had those two years of dating been about? Hannah wondered bitterly.

"The thing is, back then when I got my first corporate sponsor, I had to do things their way. Maintain a certain image."

Which, Hannah well knew, hadn't included her.

"But now that I've been in this a while, I've got a little clout with the sponsors. They're as frustrated as I am that I'm not winning as much as I should. Which is why I'd like you on my team as a consultant. No one can make a car run as fast as you."

That much, at least, was true, Hannah acknowledged. She had a talent for bringing an engine to peak condition.

"I don't think so." Hannah caught Dylan looking at her, a curious expression on his face. Not quite jealousy, but…concern, maybe? For her well-being? Grateful to find that at least some man who knew her in a romantic sense cared about her feelings, she started to move past Rupert.

Rupert caught her arm and drew her back even more urgently. "Listen, I know what you're thinking. You're worried about being around Amber so much 'cause she's always in the pit cheering me on. But you don't have to worry about that. She knows you're just a mechanic and she'll be nice to you, I swear."

Just a mechanic. It was all Hannah could do not to deck him then and there. "As I said, thanks, but no thanks." As she pushed the words through her teeth, Hannah was relieved to see Dylan had turned back to the person standing next to him, still talking animatedly. It was bad enough she was being humiliated this way without Dylan actually hearing what was being said to her.

"Just stay here and I'll go and get Amber," Rupert persisted. Catching sight of his snotty beauty-queen wife, he rushed off.

Not about to be subjected to that, Hannah headed off in the opposite direction, toward the front of the mansion. She had just rounded the corner and stepped into the broad front wall, when she heard Rupert and Amber gaining on her.

Hannah muttered an oath and dashed up the sweeping staircase to the second floor. To her increasing dismay, Amber and Rupert followed. Hannah increased her speed, going through one wing after another. And still, they were right behind her. She pushed her way through the throngs of guests milling around in some of the second-floor sitting rooms or standing in line to use the various powder rooms. Hurried down another hall where there was a staircase leading to the third or top floor, but it was cordoned off with a velvet rope barricade.

Obviously, guests were not to go up there, but desperate times called for desperate measures.

"I KNOW SHE'S UP HERE," Rupert Wallace declared.

Determined not to be found, Hannah lay very still as the door opened.

"Who cares where she is?" Amber pouted.

"I do." Rupert said, sounding highly annoyed. Finally the door shut, and their footsteps receded down the hall once again.

Hannah breathed an enormous sigh of relief.

Too soon the door to the third-floor library opened—and closed—yet again. And this time, a small lamp close to the portal was turned on before quiet, steady, unerringly male footsteps made their way across the hardwood floor.

Figuring the best defense was a good offense, Hannah closed her eyes and feigned sleep. Only to regret it as she drank in the tantalizingly familiar fragrance of man and soap and cologne.

The footsteps stopped just short of her. Hannah could feel the warmth of the tall body standing next to the long leather sofa. "Playing possum," her finder drawled, "is not going to work with me."

Chapter Five

Care to bet? Hannah thought, remaining very still.

Just because Dylan Hart wanted to know what she was up to did not mean she had to tell him.

"Okay then, Sleeping Beauty," he said, amusement in his low voice, "I'll have to rouse you some other way."

The next thing Hannah knew, Dylan had dropped to his knees beside the leather sofa. He leaned across her, his lips on hers in a light, reverential kiss suited for a fairy-tale princess. Desire swept through her, quick and urgent, and it was all she could do not to open her lips to his and initiate a deeper, sexier, much more involved kiss. But knowing full well where an action like that might lead, she opened her eyes and telegraphed a subtle delay-of-game warning instead.

His confident smile letting her know he was aware of the sudden, tremulous nature of her breathing, Dylan rose and sat down beside her, his hips next to hers. "So," he said, giving her a look that let her know this was only a warm-up to what he really wanted to do with her.

Hannah pretended an insouciance she couldn't begin to feel. "So," she echoed playfully, mocking his tone.

His posture relaxed, he covered one of her hands with her own and probed her face with a relentlessly searching glance. Suddenly serious again, he said, "Why are you hiding in here?"

Her pulse racing at his nearness, Hannah withdrew her hand from the warmth of his. *That* she did not want to discuss. "I'm not hiding," she told him stiffly, wishing there was a graceful way to extricate herself from his presence. But there wasn't unless he moved and he did not appear ready to do so, and she remained incredibly aware of him, her body throbbing all over in silent yearning.

Dylan, however, seemed only interested in his fact-finding mission. He regarded her stoically, appearing unconvinced by her denials. "Really," he told her dryly.

His suspicion only made her all the more determined to keep her embarrassment to herself. "I'm waiting for someone." As soon as the words were out, Hannah wondered where that face-saving fib had come from. And why did it matter to her so much what Dylan thought of her? Was it because she didn't want him to see her as vulnerable? Or was it her foolishness where her former love was concerned that she wanted to hide?

He narrowed his eyes at her. If Hannah didn't know better, she would think he was jealous at the idea of her rendezvousing with another man.

"Yeah, who?" Dylan demanded, looking ready to pick up the sword in her honor.

The thought of Dylan fighting to lay claim to her made Hannah happy and she shrugged. "You?" she quipped with a teasing smile.

Dylan's sober expression did not alter. "I'm serious, Hannah."

She knew he was. That was the problem. She didn't want to talk frankly about this, even as she knew Dylan wouldn't give up until he had gotten the whole sorry story out of her. Or if not her, then someone close to her. And she wasn't sure which alternative was worse. Fury rising, she pushed past him and struggled about as ungracefully as it was possible to do to get off the sofa. Once on her feet, she tugged the hem of her dress back down where it was supposed to be, just above her knees, and strode away from him, her heels making a sharp staccato sound on the polished hardwood floor. "You wouldn't understand," Hannah told him miserably, folding her arms in front of her and drawing a deep stabilizing breath.

"Sure about that?" Dylan challenged softly as he stood and moved where she had no choice but to look at him.

Yes, she was. If only because he had the kind of naturally sophisticated appearance and suave manner that was good enough to be invited anywhere, as well as to grace the television screens of hundreds of thousands of people.

"Maybe you should try me, anyway," he persisted with a gentle understanding that infuriated her all the more.

Hannah glared at Dylan as her emotions soared out of control. "I sincerely doubt that you have any idea what it's like to be humiliated the way I was when Rupert Wallace dumped me and ran off with that beauty queen. To be told, 'Gee, thanks, Hannah, you're okay to hang out with and spend hour upon hour beneath the underbelly of a car with, but you're not pretty enough or feminine or sophisticated enough to fit into my new and exciting life. In fact, I'd be downright embarrassed to be seen with you at those big parties my new NASCAR sponsors throw.'" She paused and shook her head, misery clogging her throat.

"Don't stop now," he urged her quietly. "Tell me the rest."

"It was just like when Granddaddy Reid didn't think a female could run the garage, and asked me to sell it after he passed," she said in a low husky monotone. The depth of her frustration made her whole body tense. Tears she refused to let fall stung her eyes. "It just hurts to spend all that time with someone and have them still not see you or who you really are or what you're capable of. It makes you wonder what's the point of ever revealing yourself to someone that way if you're only going to get your heart stomped on and be made a fool of in the end. And the thing with Rupert Wallace just took the cake. It made me want to never be truly vulnerable or involved with anyone again. It made me want to just compartmentalize my life—the way guys do—and put sex here and fun here and *no commitment ever* over here."

Dylan's eyes never left her face as she rambled on but she couldn't read his expression.

Hannah drew a deep breath and spit out the rest of the story before he could ask her any more questions. "So when I saw Rupert here tonight and he wanted me to be all buddy-buddy with him and the missus so he could use me all over again, after he dumped me so he could make a big to-do and marry her, it was just too much," she revealed bitterly. "So I ran off and hid and made an utter fool of myself all over again, this time with no help whatsoever from him."

Hannah stopped her tirade to take another breath. "I just hate it when someone doesn't believe in me, you know? When they spend all this time with me and still don't see me for who I am, deep down, in here." She pointed to her heart. Needing, wanting him to understand, even as she doubted that he ever really would. "Not that *you* would ever know anything about having to harden your heart so you'll never be played for a fool again, anyway."

Dylan probably had women dropping at his feet. Dylan could probably have anyone and everyone he wanted! Men that handsome and sexy and together always did.

"Don't kid yourself, Hannah," Dylan said gruffly, looking as regretful as she felt. His lips took on a grim, unyielding line as he gazed deep into her eyes. "I've had my own share of heartache and been made a damn fool of, too."

DYLAN COULD SEE THAT Hannah didn't believe him. He needed to make her understand that he did comprehend what she had been through. "It's true," he said quietly. "Soon after moving to Chicago, I got involved with a very successful lobbyist. She was beautiful and sexy and exciting and I thought she was head over heels in love with me." Dylan shook his head, recalling what an easy mark he had been. His voice dropped another regret-filled notch, "So when she suggested we run off and elope on a moment's notice, I said okay."

Hannah's eyes widened in surprise. "You got married?"

"On a cruise ship in the Bahamas."

She regarded him hesitantly, then moved forward, so close they were almost touching. "But your family never mentioned your tying the knot," she protested softly.

Dylan shoved a hand through his hair. "That's because they don't know about it."

She touched his arm. "Why not?" she asked sympathetically.

"Because," Dylan continued, wishing in hindsight he had been a little smarter in the romance department, too. "I found out while we were still on our honeymoon that Desirée was only using her marriage to me as a cover. Turns out she was really in love with a very married politician whose wife had become more than a little suspicious."

Hannah dropped her hand, stepped back a pace. "She told you this?" she queried in raging disbelief.

Dylan pressed his lips together as he related, "Yes, but only after I caught her talking with her lover on the phone. Anyway, suffice it to say," he continued with a weariness that came straight from his soul, "the marriage was over almost before it began. We agreed it would be best if no one knew about our mistake, so we got a quick and quiet divorce while we were still in the Caribbean and that was that."

Hannah struggled to take it all in. "So you've been married and divorced and no one in your family knows about it?" she murmured, stunned.

Dylan nodded, happy about this much. "And I have no plans to tell them, either, so I would appreciate it if you didn't say anything."

"Of course I won't." An awkward silence fell between them.

Dylan studied Hannah. "You think I'm making a mistake."

She shrugged her slender shoulders and moved toward the sofa again. She sat down in the center of it and braced her hands on either side of the crushed-velvet fabric. "I'm just not sure it's wise to keep something so important from your family."

"I know what I'm doing, Hannah." Pride radiated in his low voice.

Hannah tilted her head as she continued to regard him meditatively. "They could find out."

"How?" Dylan sat down beside her, so close their thighs were almost touching. "Desirée and I eloped without telling anyone what we were doing and ended it the same way. The only other person who knows—besides you—is her politician lover, and believe me, he's not going to say anything."

Hannah nodded without saying anything.

"You still think keeping the truth from my family is a mistake."

"I think sooner or later it's bound to come out, if only when you apply for a marriage license again."

"Marriage isn't in the cards for me. I made a fool of myself once. I don't plan on doing it again," Dylan finished as voices sounded in the hall. Recognizing them immediately, Hannah moaned. "Not again."

Dylan scowled his displeasure as she lay flat against the cushions once again. "I'm not hiding," he scoffed. He wasn't afraid to face Rupert Wallace with exactly what he thought of him.

Hannah grabbed his hand and dragged him down so he was lying on top of her. "The heck you're not."

Astounded and aroused to find himself in the missionary position with a woman he very much wanted to bed, Dylan grinned mischievously down at Hannah as the door opened.

"I don't recall this light being on before," Rupert said, walking in slightly.

"Oh, who cares, Rupert! We're missing the party!" Amber complained.

They moved off, shutting the door behind them.

Dylan and Hannah were still on the sofa, hearts beating wildly. "You can get up now," Hannah told him dryly.

"I could." Dylan grinned as he settled more comfortably atop her. Realizing there had never been a moment of his life he wanted to enjoy more, he captured her wrists in his hands. "And I will," he promised her suggestively, unable to help but notice just how beautiful Hannah looked, with color in her cheeks, her green eyes glittering excitedly, her auburn hair in a soft sexy cloud around her head. "But not…just…yet."

HANNAH SAW THE KISS COMING. If she was smart, she would figure out some way to avoid locking lips with him. But she wasn't wise when it came to Dylan. Never had been. And, she suspected, never would be.

His kiss was everything she had expected, and everything she hadn't. It was soft and warm and unbearably seductive. At first. Gradually, it grew harder, hotter, more demanding. So demanding that she arched her back and opened her lips and pressed her breasts against his chest. He groaned, too, then, as their tongues mated and their breaths joined and their lips fused. A feeling of femininity swept through her, intensifying the liquid desire she felt deep inside her. And she knew it was all due to Dylan. He made her feel more a woman than she ever had in her life. And she wanted to feel even more as she whispered his name and threw herself even more wholeheartedly into the erotic embrace.

And that was when the door opened again.

HANNAH WAS STILL FUMING over the interruption an hour later. "I can't believe that security guard actually told us to 'get a room'!"

Dylan shook off the remark. Unlike her, he had taken it in stride. Maybe, Hannah thought, because sexy things like that happened to Dylan every day. Whereas to her, well, to her, moments like that just didn't happen.

And that made the loss of the passionate embrace all the harder to take. Because she wasn't sure it would ever happen again.

Not when the two of them were thinking clearly, anyway.

Dylan parked his rental car in her driveway. He turned off the engine, looking as relaxed as ever. "He was just teasing us, Hannah," Dylan chided. "And you have to know we had it coming, doing what we were doing, where we were doing it."

Maybe so, Hannah conceded silently, but the guard's remark had still left her thinking, all the way back to her place, about hotel rooms and Dylan and making hot, reckless, wonderful love. Not a good thing for someone who was working so hard to protect herself.

Because if ever there was a man who could smash her heart all to pieces, it was the sumptuously seductive Dylan Hart.

"I hate to ask," Dylan told her affably as they reached her front door.

She had been hoping for another kiss. Instead, she got a matter-of-fact request.

"But would it be okay," Dylan continued, his dark brown eyes serious, "if I came in for just a minute? Just to check my e-mail. I'm fairly certain I'm going to be asked to come out and interview for this TV station in San Francisco…"

Hannah tried not to think how far away from Holly Springs that was. Even by jet, it was a good six-, seven-hour flight. Which would make quick weekend trips back to North Carolina all but impossible.

Telling herself she was getting way too far ahead of herself here, she smiled at him agreeably as Dylan took out his phone and checked. No messages. "Sure," she said as they walked toward the loft stairs, pretending she didn't have anything at all riding on this. "Go ahead."

Dylan already had his eyes on the computer. "Thanks."

"Meanwhile, I'm going to get out of this dress." Not because she was uncomfortable in the alluring sheath—to the contrary, she felt great in it—but because her breasts were spilling out of the décolletage neckline. And she didn't need to feel any more ardent and in need of romance than she already did, thanks to Dylan and his passionate kisses.

A distracted expression on his face, he was already sitting down at her desk, while she grabbed a T-shirt and cotton pajama pants and disappeared into the master bathroom.

Only to find out seconds later, to her frustration, that the zipper was not about to budge. Fearful of damaging a dress that didn't belong to her, Hannah had no choice. She came back out into the bedroom. Any hopes she might have harbored about further romance promptly faded. Dylan was staring straight ahead at the computer screen. She might as well have been standing there in her grimy mechanic's coverall instead of the most beautiful dress she had ever worn in her life.

"Anything?" Hannah asked, trying hard not to wear her heart on her sleeve.

"No," Dylan told her, clearly disappointed. "Not yet."

Hannah edged nearer, aware all over again of the deliciously masculine fragrance of Dylan's skin and hair—like soap and cologne and the unique scent that was him. "Do me a favor?" she said, her tone as casual as she could make it. As if things like this happened to *her* every day. "I'm stuck."

DYLAN HAD BEEN DOING his best to forget he was in Hannah's bedroom, or that she was in the next room, putting on something a lot more comfortable. But with her standing next to him, the desire fueled by their earlier kisses came roaring back. He had never wanted to make a woman his more than he did at that very moment. And never had such reservations about doing so. Because for Hannah, and for him, making love would be no simple fling. Despite all her brave talk about compartmentalizing her life the way guys did, he knew she wasn't the type who could ever sleep with someone without it meaning something. Nor was he. Worse, he knew if he had made her his even once, he would never be able to forget her. Never be able to walk away unscathed, as if something momentous hadn't just happened. And walk away—from her and Holly Springs—was just what he was getting ready to do.

Oblivious to his thoughts, she had already given him her back. And what a beautiful back it was. Lovely, feminine, with shoulders that were exactly the right width and shape, and silky-smooth skin that just begged for his tender touch....

"It feels like the zipper is caught in the fabric," she told him in a low, worried voice.

Dylan stood, hoping to ease the pressure at the front of his trousers, as well as the demand inside his heart that said to hell with the future, he needed to concentrate on Hannah, and the here and now.

"You're right," he said in a low, gravelly tone. "Hang on. I'll see what I can do." He tried moving the zipper with both hands on the outside of the fabric. To no avail. Another wave of desire swept through him as he said, "I'm going to have to put my hand inside your dress to get it."

She drew a quick breath at the first contact of his fingers against her skin. By the time he had worked the fabric free of the metal teeth, she was trembling, and he was equally aroused. "There," he said triumphantly, lowering the zipper another inch. Maybe they could get through this without him doing something less than chivalrous after all.

"Thank goodness," Hannah laughed softly. "I thought we were going to have to call the EMTs to come and cut me out of the dress."

Dylan smiled, not trusting himself to speak. Hannah disappeared into the bathroom again, only to come out a minute later, red-faced. "You're not going to believe this," she said.

She had gotten the zipper caught again. This time just below her bra strap. Which—dear God—was made of some transparent and shimmering gold-mesh fabric. Fighting the instantaneous reaction of his body, Dylan motioned her all the way around. Once again, he slid one hand between the fabric and her soft, warm skin, delighting in the womanly feel of her. She sucked in a breath at the intimate contact. And heaven help him, Dylan knew exactly how she felt, as he struggled, a lot less efficiently this time, to free the fussy zipper.

When at last the fabric was disengaged from the metal teeth once again, Hannah said in a low, strained voice, "Maybe you'd better draw it all the way down for me this time."

"Good idea," Dylan said.

The only problem was, drawing it all the way down let him see even more of her bare silky skin, as well as the rest of her undergarments, which turned out to be a thong and garter belt in the same transparent gold-mesh fabric as her bra.

It was all he could do to stifle a moan.

"Thanks." Hannah shot him a hurried look over her shoulder, then another, longer one. The next thing Dylan knew, she was turning all the way toward him. The look in her eyes was the same he imagined was in his.

"I promised myself I wasn't going to do this," Hannah said, already going up on tiptoe.

"What?" Dylan rasped, wondering if anything had ever felt so good. He wrapped his arms around her as she snuggled up against him.

"Make a fool of myself over you," she murmured as she threaded her fingers through his hair and pressed her breasts against his chest.

And all similar promises of chivalrous restraint were history.

"If that's what this is," Dylan murmured back just as playfully, allowing her to direct his mouth to hers, "count me in."

As their lips fused, Dylan's body ignited and so did his soul. He realized he wanted her to surrender to him, to this, heart and soul. And he could feel her melting against him, even as her spirit remained as feisty and independent as ever. Determined to make this night the most memorable one she had ever had, he backed her up against the wall so his hips pressed into hers. He leaned in even closer, engulfing her with the heat and strength of his body. He kissed her again and she moaned as he rained kisses down her throat, across her cheeks, before zeroing in on her mouth once again. Her lips parted beneath the pressure of his and he delighted in the sweet, hot taste of her.

Dylan was just easing the dress off her shoulders, when his cell phone rang. Scowling at the interruption, he pulled it out of his pocket and shut it off entirely without even looking to see who was calling him. Right now all he cared about was Hannah. "Now, where were we?" he whispered, tossing the phone aside.

Her eyes glowed ardently. "Right here." Hannah let the dress fall all the way to the floor, then stepped out of it and set it on a chair.

"Wow," Dylan said as he let his eyes drift over her. Her breasts were round and full, the pouting nipples rosy and perfect. Her waist was slender, her hips nicely curved, the feminine part of her just as delicate.

She looked up at him shyly. "You're not just saying that?"

So aroused he could barely contain himself, Dylan shook his head, stunned she could doubt herself on any level, never mind this! "Are you kidding?" he demanded hoarsely, treating himself to another long, arousing look. "A more beautiful and sexy woman was never made. And if you need proof…" He took her hand and held it against him.

Her eyes widened at the heat and size of him. She grinned, impressed. "Wow."

He looked deep into her eyes, beginning to realize just how much fun this was going to be. "You're not just teasing me?"

She took his hand in hers and kissed the back of it. "A more perfect man was never made."

Her hot-blooded perusal certainly made him feel that way. "Then what do you say we take all this perfection—"

"And head for the sheets?" Hannah was already one step ahead of him.

"My thoughts exactly." He watched her pause to take off her shoes, noting her legs were just as sexy out of heels as in them.

"Dylan?" Hannah perched on the edge of the bed as he took off his suit jacket, tie, began undoing the cuff links on his shirt.

Damn, but she was gorgeous in those undies…. "Hmm?"

Color flooded her cheeks as their eyes met once again. "You don't have to wait for me."

Dylan blinked, stunned by the inference that this

was going to turn into some slam-bam-thank-you-ma'am. "Like hell I don't," he said gruffly. Realizing from the uncertain look in her eyes that this was more about her than him now.

"What I mean to say is…" She paused, raked her teeth across her lower lip and swallowed hard. She met his eyes with difficulty. "I'm not sure I can. And I—I feel it's only fair to say that at the outset…so there's no—no misunderstanding later."

Aware the last thing he wanted from her was a stammering apology in advance, Dylan shed his trousers, shirt and socks before joining her on the bed. He would have preferred to be naked, but the nervousness in her expression had him keeping his black silk racer-style briefs on. Amazed she seemed to have no clue how sensually responsive a woman she was, he took her hand in his and asked her gently, "Can't or never have?"

Her blush told the sad tale.

Dylan shook his head, aware they were both about to head into "virgin" territory. "Then it's because no one has ever treated you right," he told her determinedly, guiding her down onto the pillows. He stretched out beside her. "I'm here to treat you right."

Hannah had been trying to save them both some embarrassment, even as she braced herself to be ultimately disappointed, but Dylan saw it as a challenge he was more than ready to take on. "Relax,

Hannah," he told her as he took her in his arms once again and pressed her against the length of his well-muscled body. "Nothing's going to happen that you're not completely ready for."

The next thing she knew, their mouths were locked in a searingly gentle kiss. He brought her so close, they were touching in one long, electrified line, then moved so she was beneath him once again. And still he kissed her, again and again, until she knew she wanted him more than life. Eyes dark with mischief and affection, he peeled off her bra and cupped her breasts in his hands. Kissing first one nipple, then the other, he worked them both to aching buds before moving lower still. Then he took off her thong, leaving the garter and stockings. Then his hands were beneath her, cupping her bottom, tugging her to the edge of the bed.

He slipped to the floor and knelt between her knees, kissing his way up her thighs until she was arching up off the bed. Moaning her pleasure, she gripped his shoulders, not sure whether she was trying to bring him closer or hold him at bay. She only knew she had never done anything like this. Never felt anything so wickedly sensual and wonderful. It felt so good to be wanted, touched. So good to let all her inhibitions fall away, and just feel him kissing her there.... And there... And there...

And then she was quaking inside, her whole world

spinning, her body exploding and coming apart from the inside out. The lightning zigzagging through her was as incredible and overpowering as her feelings for him. And yet she still wanted so much more. She whimpered low in her throat, the yearning inside her fierce and unquenchable. "Dylan—" Her hands tightened on his shoulders. She wanted him to climax, too. The sooner, the better.

"We're getting there," he teased as he rejoined her on the bed. He moved on top of her, still kissing her hotly and rapaciously.

Impatient now to have him experience the same wonderful pleasure, Hannah slid her hands inside his briefs and found his sex as abundant and silky hot as she expected it to be. Together, they freed him, and he moved atop of her once again.

"Now," Hannah breathed, still quaking from the aftershocks of her earlier climax. "Oh, Dylan, I want you. So much."

"Hannah, Hannah, I want you, too." Hands beneath her, he cupped her bottom, and lifted her toward him, spreading her thighs. She opened herself to him as he took her slowly, sweetly. Their mating as slow and sensual and deep as their earlier kisses. Until the fire flared out of control, and they were both moaning, straining, as she took him deeper and deeper inside her and they shared soft kisses and hard kisses and kisses that fell in between. And then there was no more holding back and she was shuddering again, and so was he, and all coherent thought spun away in ribbons of endless pleasure.

Afterward, they clung together, the pinnacle of passion leaving them exhausted and replete. Dylan tenderly stroked her hair and kissed her temple. "Now, what were you saying about not being able to climax?"

She grinned and kissed him again. "No longer a problem."

He regarded her with barely checked affection. "I should say not," he told her.

Hannah sobered, thinking about what he had given her. "Thank you," she said softly.

"For…?"

"Showing me how much a woman I am. I needed that." *I needed you. I needed to feel wonderful and desired and capable of a lifelong love and you gave me all of that. And regardless of what does or does not happen next, I'll have the memory of this night to keep with me forever.*

An emotion she couldn't quite decipher gleamed in his eyes. "Well, don't thank me yet," he told her huskily. "We're not done."

Hannah had known, theoretically anyway, that sex could be very physically satisfying. What she hadn't expected was to feel so emotionally connected, too. But she did. And judging from the expression on his face, Dylan was feeling pretty close to her right now, too.

Close enough to want to stay the night with her, it appeared....

"We're just getting started, Hannah." His lips curved in masculine satisfaction and he regarded her in a way that reminded her what a demanding and giving lover he had been. "Trust me." Dylan looked deep into her eyes. *"We're just getting started."*

Chapter Six

Hannah woke, snuggled in Dylan's arms. As the events of the night before came flooding back to her, it was all she could do not to groan out loud. What had seemed like a great idea the night before now seemed very foolish indeed.

Hannah had never been a reckless person, but she had made love with Dylan as if there were no tomorrow. Forgetting that he was going to be leaving again in just a few days.

And yet, Hannah thought as she slowly and cautiously eased out of the light protective grasp of Dylan's naked body, and moved away from the bed, she couldn't in all honesty say she regretted the lovemaking that had brought her such incredible pleasure and left her feeling—for those few precious hours anyway—like the most cherished woman on earth.

But now it was daylight again, and the workday

dawned. She needed to pull herself together before she faced a wide-awake Dylan.

Hannah slipped into the T-shirt and pajama pants she had meant to put on the evening before, belted a calf-length cotton robe over that, and went downstairs to the construction zone on the first floor. She put some coffee on to brew, then went out to get the newspaper.

Unfortunately, no sooner had she walked to the curb and bent down to pick it up, than a familiar black-and-white patrol car pulled up, and—to her mortification—stopped.

Dylan's older brother, Sheriff Mac Hart, got out. He tipped the brim of his khaki-colored hat at her. "Hannah."

"Mac."

"I hate to ask—" Mac glanced at the rental car parked in Hannah's driveway, then back at her "—but is my brother Dylan here, perchance?"

Hannah swallowed. Talk about embarrassing! She dipped her head in acknowledgment. "Did you need to speak to him?" she asked politely.

Mac nodded. "If it wouldn't be too much trouble." He paused respectfully. "I can wait out here if you like."

"Don't be silly. I just put some coffee on." She waved Mac on in as casually as if he stopped by at this hour every day. She already saw blinds move in the house across the street and didn't want to attract any more attention from the neighbors.

Mac kept the conversation on friendly, cordial terms as they walked inside and came face-to-face with Dylan.

Oblivious to the fact they were about to have company, he was standing there in nothing but a pair of black silk bikini briefs, pouring himself a cup of coffee. Dylan didn't look pleased when he saw Mac, but he didn't try to hide what had been going on, either. Not that he could have, Hannah realized ruefully, feeling hideously embarrassed to more or less have been caught in the act.

"A little early for a social call, isn't it?" Dylan gave Mac an even glance that spoke volumes about Dylan's resentment at the intrusion.

Which, Hannah noted, Mac promptly ignored. "Mom has been looking for you," Mac stated matter-of-factly. "She didn't tell me why, but she is clearly on the warpath. More so now because you didn't come back to my place last night."

Dylan scowled. "And how would she know that?" he challenged.

"Because," Mac sighed, sounding exasperated at having been put in the middle of this, "I told her I'd have you call her no matter how late you got in and you never called. She's a bright woman, Dylan, more than able to put two and two together!"

Dylan shoved his hands through the rumpled layers of his sandy hair. "Why didn't you tell me this last night?"

"I tried," Mac retorted just as contentiously. "You weren't answering your cell phone."

Hannah flushed, recalling very well the moment Dylan had shut off the phone, and never turned it back on. "You know what?" She forced cheer into her voice. "I'm going to leave you two to hash this out while I go up and get a shower."

"Good idea," Dylan muttered. He looked at Mac. "Coming here wasn't."

Mac muttered something in return that Hannah couldn't quite catch as she headed up the loft stairs and into the bathroom. No sooner had she shut the door behind her than the conversation downstairs continued, more frankly than ever.

"What the hell are you doing," Mac asked Dylan in a hushed angry voice. "Putting the moves on her? Damn it all, Dylan, we told you to dance with her, not…"

The blood draining out of her face, Hannah perched on the edge of the tub. Obviously, the two brothers didn't realize how well sound carried in the half-renovated house. Nor had she until this very moment….

"What are you trying to say, Mac?" Dylan volleyed back, sounding even more annoyed.

"Exactly what you think I'm saying," Mac countered. "That it's obvious Hannah Reid is not your type."

YOU WOULDN'T SAY THAT if you had seen her last night, Dylan thought. Hannah had knocked 'em all dead in that dress…

And you wouldn't say that if you had kissed her, and made love to her, either. But not about to go into all that with his Dudley Do-Right older brother, Dylan only said, "Hannah knows where we stand."

"And where exactly is that?" Mac grilled Dylan relentlessly.

"Hannah and I are friends," Dylan said flatly.

"Friends?" Mac echoed in disbelief.

Dylan struggled to explain a situation he was just beginning to comprehend himself. "She doesn't have anyone in her life right now. Neither do I." That made them lonely, vulnerable. But it was more than that. Dylan couldn't explain it. Just thinking it sounded a little hokey. But he had this feeling that somehow he and Hannah were meant to be. That his losing his job, being here with her when it happened, was somehow fated. That it was all part of a larger plan to bring them together. But he knew if he tried telling any of that to his "Just the facts, please!" older brother he'd be laughed out of the room.

Mac saw things in black and white. Right and wrong.

"So that justifies you taking her to bed?" Mac was incensed.

A little hard to deny when he was standing there in his briefs, and Mac had just seen Hannah in her pajamas. Dylan quaffed his coffee and continued looking at Mac. He refused to feel ashamed about something so beautiful. "I want her to feel appreciated," Dylan said finally. *I want Hannah to know that she can be whatever she wants to be with me… one of the guys…the woman in my arms and my bed and my life….*

But Mac was still stuck on what he had just said out loud. "Appreciated," Mac repeated, sounding even angrier. He looked at Dylan as if he didn't know whether to throttle him or throw up his hands in disgust and leave. "So what happened here last night was an act of mercy on your part?" Mac leaned in close to give Dylan the full benefit of his censuring glare. "Is that what you're telling me?"

Put like that it didn't sound very good, Dylan thought.

Maybe he should just shut up now.

Leave it at that.

Mac shook his head in mute aggravation. "I hope you know what you're doing," he swore, sounding at that moment more father than brother to Dylan.

Dylan folded his arms in front of him. He knew

how it looked. He also knew he would never do anything to hurt Hannah, and hence, had nothing to feel sorry about.

Dylan looked Mac straight in the eye. "I know exactly what I'm doing."

But to Dylan's consternation, Mac still didn't believe it. And he certainly didn't approve. "Call Mom." Mac compressed his lips grimly and straightened the brim of his hat as he looked at Dylan long and hard. "Whatever it is she wants to talk to you about isn't going to wait."

HANNAH HEARD DYLAN coming up the loft stairs. Knowing if she didn't face him now she would never be able to face him, she walked out of the bathroom clad exactly as she had been before. Dylan took one look at her face and knew she'd heard absolutely everything that had just been said.

"Is it true?" Hannah asked, feeling like a fool because she'd thought that she and Dylan had started something fantastic. Okay, maybe they weren't headed for marriage, but she had thought their lovemaking meant something to him. Now, thanks to Mac's sheriff-like interrogation, she knew differently. "Did your brothers tell you to dance with me?" she asked in a low, bewildered voice.

"Yes." Dylan reached for his clothes and began to dress. Pants first, then his shirt. He looked at her as if his brother's request was the most natural occurrence in the world. "At Janey's wedding."

She watched as he sat down to put on his socks and shoes. "And yet you never asked me to dance that night," she recalled.

He ran a comb through his hair, restoring order to the rumpled sand-colored strands. "I tried near the end of the reception but you were nowhere to be found."

It was her turn to feel guilty as Hannah realized where she probably had been, and with whom. "How much easier it would be for both of us now if you could have found me that night," she said, shaking her head bitterly.

Looking a lot more in control now than he had when Mac had arrived and caught them both in a state of undress, Dylan held out both hands imploringly. "Hannah—"

"It's all right, Dylan." Hannah held up both hands to ward him off. "You and I both know what happened here last night."

Dylan edged even closer. Refusing to let her off the hook, he took her all the way into his arms. "And what was that?"

Hannah swallowed around the growing knot of emotion in her throat. She felt humiliated and embarrassed. But she'd be damned if she would be a coward, too. She looked Dylan straight in the eye and called it what it obviously was. "We both indulged in a mercy—"

Dylan cut her off before she could finish the crude slang term. "That's not true and you know it," he said angrily.

"Isn't it?" Hannah asked wearily, determined to lay all their cards on the table. "You made me climax for the first time in my life. I don't know about you, Dylan, but I'd say that was pretty merciful."

"Hannah—" Dylan began.

She extricated herself from his embrace. "Not that it matters in any case. For starters, you're going to be out of here as soon as you find a job, and we both knew that from the get-go. And secondly," Hannah said, knowing from years of experience working in a man's world that the best way to put a man at ease in a tricky situation was to behave exactly the way a guy would behave. "It's obvious that what happened last night was a rebound thing for both of us."

Dylan blinked in stunned amazement, falling for her face-saving device hook, line and sinker. "How do you get that?" he asked, sounding both wary and angry.

Hannah shrugged as she disappeared into the bathroom to get dressed, too. "I had a run-in with my ex-boyfriend." She spoke through the slit in the mostly closed door.

Dylan moved off. Hannah was glad he had the grace to give her the privacy she needed.

"I didn't see my ex last night," Dylan said from a distance away.

Jeans and work shirt on, Hannah emerged from the bathroom. Dylan was seated at her desk, already booting up her laptop. "But you talked about her. And resurrecting all that embarrassment and humiliation made us want to seek comfort. Which we found," Hannah said in her best, one-night-stand voice. Which, unfortunately for the believability of the moment, she had never used before. "And that's okay, Dylan." She sat down on the edge of the bed to put on her socks and shoes, glad her bravado was working, because if it hadn't been, she just might have had to dissolve into tears.

"Because we both know a fling is all last night was." She glanced at the open laptop on her desk. "So what's happening?" she continued casually, as if she weren't as heartbroken as she had ever been. As if he weren't sitting there, looking as frustrated and angry and tired of talking about all this and examining it to death as she felt.

If only they'd left this situation the way it was when she woke up, as something new and wonderful that didn't bear looking at too closely. Yet, anyway. If only they could have gone on just enjoying and appreciating and really getting to know each other a little while longer…

But Mac's interruption, and their crash landing in

the real world, had ended all romance and fantasy. And now, Hannah realized wearily, as Dylan obviously already had, the two of them just had to deal. She swallowed hard. "Any news on the job front?"

Busy reading down a highlighted list of new messages, Dylan nodded. He pointed to the computer screen. "The TV station in San Francisco wants me out there next Monday. I'm going to sub for the regular sportscaster on Tuesday. That will serve as my audition for the spot."

Hannah didn't have to pretend to be impressed about that—she admired the quick way Dylan seemed to be landing on his feet. Jobwise, anyway.

"Great." She paused, and forced herself to be even more cordial and adult about the situation. Because she knew she owed him that. He hadn't made her any false promises. Or tried to string her along. They had made love the night before because they had both wanted to. Period. As an adult woman, she had to deal with that. She looked at him sincerely. "I hope you get the job."

Something in him softened. "Thanks," he said just as quietly.

Downstairs, the doorbell rang again. "That's probably the painters," Dylan said with a beleaguered sigh, looking as uneager as it was possible to be. He rose with the grace of a tiger on the prowl. "I'll let them in."

BUT IT WASN'T THE painters, Dylan realized unhappily. It was the person he least wanted to see. He stopped just short of barring the door. "Mom, this is not a good time," he said.

"I'll bet it's not," Helen Hart said. Brushing by him, she came right on in and looked past him. "Hello, Hannah."

A second string of swearwords echoed in Dylan's head. Hannah would have been better served to simply seek cover and stay put than endure this.

"Hello, Mrs. Hart," Hannah said sweetly.

Helen turned back to Dylan. She was dressed for work in a pastel business suit, her short red hair perfectly arranged, her amber eyes unerringly direct. "Why didn't you tell me?" she demanded, upset, looking at fifty-six as trim and energetic as she had in Dylan's youth. Unfortunately she wasn't about to cut him any more slack when it came to his behavior than she did her other five grown children. She strode closer, her high heels clicking on the hardwood floor. "Why did I have to hear it from family friends in Chicago?"

"Hear what?" Dylan poured his mother a cup of coffee as he stalled for time.

Helen shook her head no, thanks, and continued looking at him as if he had lost his mind. "That you've been fired!"

Still stalling, Dylan handed the coffee to Hannah, then poured himself a cup, too.

Helen looked around and finally perched on one of the sawhorses littering the construction area. "Dylan, for heaven's sake! We could have supported you in what has to be a very terrible time."

Dylan took a sip and found the coffee hot but bitter. "I'm doing all right. I already have several irons in the fire."

"I'm sure you do, but that doesn't fix the problem between us." Helen regarded Dylan sternly.

Aware Hannah was watching the familial exchange with interest, Dylan did his best to contain his temper. "There is no problem," he said evenly.

Helen arched a skeptical eyebrow. "There *is* a problem if you think it's okay to shut me and the rest of your family out like this."

"Speaking of family," Hannah interrupted, uncomfortable, "I'm not really…so I think I'll just mosey on out of here."

Dylan stopped her before she could reach her shoulder bag and keys. "You don't have to go, Hannah." He tossed a pointed look at his mother. "Mom was just leaving. Weren't you, Mom?"

Helen stood, gracious as ever. Polite. But not done in. "We are not finished here, Dylan."

"Yes, we are." Dylan put down his coffee mug and escorted Helen out the door, to her car. And there, to Dylan's chagrin, his mother really let him have it.

"I understand you have a wounded ego in response to your job loss. But romancing Hannah is no way to fix that."

Guilt flashed through Dylan, followed swiftly by denial. "My going after her has nothing to do with me feeling bad about losing my job."

"I might believe that," Helen said wearily, abruptly looking as exasperated as he felt, "if you hadn't followed the same pattern after your dad died."

The facade of coping just fine in the wake of the most major loss of his life—save his dad's death—began to crack just a little. Dylan swallowed hard around the sudden ache in his throat. "I don't know what you're talking about."

Her eyes gentled and she gazed at him in the way that said she understood him better than he knew, always had and always would. "That was when you started watching televised sports nonstop."

Dylan swallowed hard and turned his attention to the front of Hannah's house. "I watched so many sports after Dad died because I loved watching games with him, when he was alive. Continuing the tradition he started with me was simply my way of comforting myself, in lieu of the loss, of keeping the gift he gave me alive—which was a love of all things athletic."

His mother touched his arm compassionately. "Exactly."

Dylan looked into her eyes, needing her to understand. "And it was a natural thing, because I was destined to do the work I am doing, Mom. Watching all sorts of games, learning about the teams and players and the owners and the records and the history of the sport, was simply a part of that."

"And," Helen added meaningfully, "it kept you from feeling the pain of your loss. Just like, I'm willing to bet, your whatever this is with Hannah is keeping you from dwelling on the loss of your job in Chicago."

"YOU LOOK TICKED OFF," Hannah noted when Dylan finally came back inside.

He *was* ticked off. His mother had not just questioned his integrity where Hannah was concerned. She had also come right out and said she doubted that his attraction to Hannah was real because he had never acted on his interest in the feisty mechanic before.

Dylan looked at Hannah, who was perched on a sawhorse eating a sweet roll and drinking a cup of coffee. He couldn't tell if she was upset or not. She was certainly acting as if all was right with her world. "This is exactly why I do not want to live around here," he told her furiously as he walked over to help himself to coffee. He hated feeling vulnerable. And his mother had made him feel very vulnerable. Worse, Hannah had witnessed it.

Hannah shrugged. "I think it's kind of nice the way they all interfere in your life. Or try to. My Granddaddy Reid—"

"What?"

"Well, he was perfectly happy to talk sports and current events and even car engines with me, but he never wanted to talk about the personal stuff." Hannah sighed.

Realizing life hadn't been a bed of roses for her, either, Dylan sat down beside her. "So you had no one to go to for advice."

"Except my childhood friends." Hannah's lower lip curved wryly. "And you can imagine how off base a lot of those words of wisdom were. And your mother's right about one thing—you shouldn't shut your family out. And that goes double when something bad happens to you, because whether you admit it or not, their moral support would probably make you feel a lot better."

Hannah had already given him all the emotional backup he needed, and then some. Even before they had torn down another barrier and made love. But not wanting to get into all that for fear it would sound cheesy, he merely shrugged and said, "A guy's got to have his pride."

"Yeah?" Hannah studied his face. "And at what cost, Dylan?"

HANNAH'S WORDS STAYED with Dylan the rest of the morning while the painting crew finished spray painting the ceiling and interior walls. They finished shortly before noon. Knowing the cabinet-installation guys weren't due to come until later in the week, Dylan decided it might be a good time to make it up to Hannah. He'd been a little short with her before she left for work that morning, when he knew she was only trying to help. So he headed over to the garage, intending to take her to lunch.

"Not here," Slim said.

Too late, Dylan realized he should have called first instead of simply taking for granted she'd be around to see him whenever he could fit her into his schedule. "Where'd she go—do you know?"

Slim continued working. "Some ritzy steakhouse next to the RDU airport."

That sounded extravagant for someone who was allegedly counting her pennies so she could finish her renovation sooner rather than later. "For lunch?"

Slim removed a rubber hose from the engine. He frowned at the split running halfway up one side. "Some guy called and asked her to meet him there. So she got all gussied up and off she went."

Dylan frowned. "You mean she changed clothes."

"Yeah. She keeps extra clothes and makeup and stuff in her office locker." Slim opened a plastic package and took out a new hose. "What's it to you, anyway?"

Dylan shrugged, pretty sure Hannah was not ready to go public with her affair with him. Although when it came down to it, he wasn't sure he would mind. If only because it might make her see what they had shared did not have to be a one-night stand.

"I was just hoping to ask her to grab something to eat with me. Guess I'm too late." Dylan shrugged again and fished for a little more information. "I didn't realize she, uh, socialized during the noon hour. I figured she'd just grab a sandwich somewhere in town, somewhere quick, or eat here at the garage."

"That'd be the norm," Slim agreed, taking pity on Dylan's genuinely lovestruck expression. "At least until of late."

Dylan watched Slim install the new hose. "What's happened lately?"

"She's gone off like this several times. Always after some guy calls. I asked her if it was someone special and she just laughed it off and turned all red, and said, 'Nah, I'm never getting married.'"

An alarm went off inside Dylan's head. "No idea who my—ah—competition might be?" Dylan asked, deciding to lay all his cards on the table in hopes of getting more complete information.

Slim shook his head. "Not a clue. All I know is that she was just beaming when she took off out of here." Slim paused, shook his head, his fondness for Hannah showing. "I hadn't seen her that excited in a long time."

THIRTY MINUTES LATER, Dylan pulled into the parking lot of the Capitol City Steakhouse. Hannah's minivan was in the lot, all right. And so were about fifty other cars.

He found a space at the very end of the lot, near the back of the restaurant, and got out of his car. He figured he would go inside, scope things out, maybe even leave before she knew he had been there. He just needed to know what was going on with her. If she had been more serious than he knew when she had said her experience with Rupert Wallace had made her want to compartmentalize her life.

Dylan was just rounding the corner, when the swinging double doors opened and a familiar figure came striding out, headed quickly in the other direction. The man was whistling happily, already putting a cell phone to his ear. What the heck was Cal doing here? Surely his married brother had not been here on some sort of rendezvous with Hannah? Had he?

Deciding he needed all the facts before he tried quizzing Cal—the most notoriously private of all the Hart brothers—on the goings-on between Cal and Hannah, Dylan stepped inside the steakhouse.

It was dark and cool, in contrast to the shimmering August heat outside, and it took a moment for his eyes to adjust. The hostess smiled at him. "May I help you?"

"I'm meeting someone," Dylan said. "I think they're already here." He glanced around the corner, past the salad bar. No Hannah there. Past the bar. Also not there. To the other dining room. Emerging from the powder room at the rear, Hannah stepped out. She was wearing a skirt again—a short denim number that made the most of her long, sexy legs, sandals and a sleeveless yellow V-necked top. She wasn't wearing much makeup, but she didn't need it. With her bright eyes and glowing skin and full soft lips, she was easily the most beautiful woman in the room.

Until she saw him standing there, anyway. Then her step faltered for just a moment, and the color left her face.

Reminded of another time…another woman… and a similar situation that had not raised his suspicions…not at first anyway, Dylan ignored the knot in his gut and plastered a smile on his face. *Hannah was not Desirée.* "Hey," he said, issuing the standard Carolina greeting.

"Hey yourself." Hannah walked up and bussed him on the cheek, as casually as if they met this way every day. "What are you doing here?" She linked her arm through his as they walked out into the lobby.

Then she let go. Looking up at him expectantly, innocence mired with the guilt in her pretty eyes.

"I was looking for a friend of mine but he's not here yet," Dylan fibbed. "What about you?"

"Same thing," Hannah said just as casually, and this time she looked as if she was telling the truth. "I was here to have lunch with a friend."

Yeah, but what friend? "Anyone I know?" Dylan asked casually.

Hannah hesitated so slightly, he might not have noticed it if his suspicions hadn't already been aroused. She shook her head and sidestepped the question completely. "Listen, I've got to go."

"Back to the shop?" Dylan couldn't help but note Hannah seemed in as much of a hurry as Cal.

"Eventually. I have a few things to take care of first. It was nice seeing you, Dylan." She touched his arm gently once again in what seemed a reluctant goodbye, then rushed off without once looking back.

"OH MY GOSH," Hannah said when she finally got home around nine-thirty that evening. She looked around the construction zone. "I knew it was going to look good painted beach-white. But I couldn't really envision it." She cast her glance up at the rafters and over the rest of the walls. "It's actually starting to look like the interior of a house now and not just some demolition area."

Dylan nodded. He, too, was pleased by the work that had been done in her absence. The central living area of the house now looked sophisticated and welcoming, open and airy. It would be a great place to hang out. He could imagine lazy days, and even better nights. Building fires in the fireplace. Heck, maybe once the kitchen was done, they could both even learn to cook. Entertain together. Whoa! Since when did he suddenly think of them in terms of "we"?

Hannah glanced back at Dylan. She looked tired but cheerful. And so innocent at heart he felt remorseful for even suspecting her of doing anything immoral or adulterous. His gut told him the Hannah standing in front of him was just not like that.

"Have you eaten dinner yet?" Unable to stop looking at the work that had been done thus far, she turned her back to him.

"No," Dylan murmured as he paused to admire her slender silhouette. He had been waiting around for her, hoping she would show up. Only to have her get here and once again treat him as just one of the guys she routinely hung out with.

"Want to go to the sports bar and catch a few games?" she asked casually.

Not exactly what he'd had in mind, Dylan thought ruefully. Him and her and fifty other admiring guys, all of whom would want her opinion on the latest trades and scores and team strategies. With everyone vying to place bets and trade quips with her, he'd be lucky to get in a word edgewise.

And he wanted a lot more than a simple word with Hannah. He wanted her to confide in him—of her own volition, no less—exactly what it was she had been up to with Cal. And then he wanted her to swear off any such activities with Cal or anyone else, entirely. From now till forever. "We could go somewhere nicer, quieter, if you like," he suggested, aware he hadn't done much for her thus far, in the courtship department, but all that was about to change, too.

Hannah shot him an odd look, misunderstanding his reasoning. "Don't be silly. I love the food at the sports bar!"

So did Dylan. But that wasn't the point. Getting so close to her she'd never be able to forget him was.

Her gaze cut to his. Oblivious to the romantic nature of his thoughts, she gave him a reassuring pat on the forearm, one buddy to another. "Forget about all that stuff I said last night, at the fund-raiser," she told him, utterly content in a way she hadn't been the evening before. "I'm comfortable being me."

Chapter Seven

"I'm a little tipsy, aren't I?" Hannah said as he helped her out of the passenger seat and onto the sidewalk in front of her house.

Dylan tried not to notice how sensational her legs looked in the short denim skirt as he wrapped a steadying arm about her waist, and when she still faltered, brought her all the way against him.

"Just a tad," he murmured in reply, aware he was now close enough to inhale the sexy hyacinth of her perfume.

"I don't know how it happened," Hannah continued to complain.

Dylan did—he never should have let them start drinking that pitcher of beer while they were waiting for their food. By the time the man-size platter of hot wings, nachos and Chinese veggie wraps with dipping sauce had come, Hannah had been well into her second beer. The jalapeño pepper on the nachos had her guzzling more. Before Dylan knew it, she was giggling wildly, at nothing in particular. And he knew he had to get her home before she followed through on her wish to order another pitcher to put out the fire still burning in her mouth.

"I can always hold my liquor," she announced quite soberly, swaying a little on her feet.

"I'm sure you can," Dylan murmured, trying not to think how soft and warm her breasts felt as they brushed against his arm. Or how nice the rest of her had felt, either. He was going to take her upstairs, put her to bed and get out of there before he lost all sense of propriety. Because right now his thoughts were not the least bit chivalrous. "Where are your keys?" Dylan demanded gruffly, irritated he couldn't seem to think about anything but taking her to bed and making hot, wild love to her all over again.

One night of ill-advised passion with her, he was beginning to realize, had not been nearly enough. And given the ardent way she was looking at him whenever she thought he didn't see, she was thinking the same.

"They're in here." Hannah swung her purse around until it connected with his middle. "Whoops." She put her hand to her lips. "Sorry 'bout that."

"I'm sure you are." Dylan sighed. What would have been his fantasy ten years ago was now his cross to bear. "Can you find them?"

Hannah shrugged. She dug around in the bottom of her purse, causing a number of things to spill out over the top and onto the sidewalk. Holding her with one hand, Dylan bent down to get them. Picking up billfold, eye drops, lipstick, tissues. No keys. But there appeared to be a lot left in her leather shoulder bag.

"May I?"

She smiled at him lopsidedly as she handed it over for his perusal. "Be my guest," she said, then broke into song. "'Be my guest. Be my guest. Be my guest...'"

"Shh." Dylan put his finger to her lips, aware she lived in a neighborhood now populated mostly by people her grandfather's age. He leaned forward to whisper in her ear and ended up brushing his lips across her temple, too. "It's after midnight," he said.

She wrapped both her arms around his waist and held on. "So?" She offered him an unrepentant grin that upped his pulse even more.

Dylan held her purse to the side as she rested her head against his chest, the same way she had after they'd made love. Pushing the erotic images that had haunted him ever since out of his mind, Dylan whispered back kindly, "So everyone around here appears to be asleep. We don't want to wake them." Dylan reached in her purse, scavenged the bottom and pulled out her keys.

"Aha!" She continued to lean on him like a drunken sailor holding on to a mast. "Found 'em."

Dylan shook his head, aware that the feel of her soft breasts brushing up and down his chest was enough to arouse a saint, and he was no saint.

Ignoring what was going on down below, he said, "Let's just get you inside."

"Okay." Her cooperation ensured, she whispered loudly, too.

"And upstairs." Dylan unlocked the door and steered her inside, past the heavy sheets of protective plastic still draped over the floor, toward the loft.

"And into bed," he continued firmly. To heck with undressing her. She could undress herself in the morning. Because if he started that, well, there was no telling what would happen. Especially with her in such a…happy…state of mind.

Hannah sat on the edge of the bed, knees slightly apart, denim skirt riding up her thighs. Dear sweet heaven, he thought, turning his glance away. He really had to get out of here before he gave in to desire and did something they would both regret.

"You're irritated with me, aren't you?" she said, looking up at him, all sweetness and angelic innocence once again.

"No," Dylan fibbed, forcing himself to meet her gaze and not think about how well that soft yellow cotton hugged her breasts, or how sexy her bare arms and shoulders looked in the sleeveless V-necked top. He

returned his gaze to the shimmering emerald depths
of her eyes and found them even more dangerous.

"Yes you are, and I want to know why you're
ticked off," Hannah insisted, deliberately and will-
fully holding his gaze.

Because, Dylan thought, she was up to something—possibly with his married brother—and he
couldn't figure out what. He didn't want to think it
could possibly have anything to do with the break-
down of Cal's marriage to Ashley. And he didn't know
how to get the information out of her that would,
hopefully, put his mind at ease without accusing her
of something she might not actually have done.

Hannah blinked in confusion, and rushed on, still
eager to understand. "Is it because I didn't show up
for dinner until 9:30?" she said, searching his face.
"And I was gone all day, too, to parts unknown?"

Talk about hitting the nail on the head!

Not about to let the chance go by to get to the heart
of the matter, Dylan sat down beside her. "Let's talk
about that," he said.

Hannah made a face, shutting him out as quickly
as she had nearly let him in. "Let's not." She lay
across the middle of the bed, one arm thrown across
her forehead. Her feet were still on the floor, her
knees still slightly apart, and Dylan was achingly
aware of how he had knelt there, before her, the night
before.

He was strong.

But not that strong.

Dylan sighed and ran a hand over his face. Saints, protect me. "Hannah—" *Help us both do what's right here.*

She touched his forearm and commanded with a candor he didn't expect, "Kiss me, Dylan. Kiss me like you kissed me last night."

Heart racing, he leaned over, hands braced on either side of her, and planted a chaste one on her, intending for that to be their good-night.

She frowned her displeasure as he started to move ever so chivalrously away from her. "Nice try, Mr. TV Man," she drawled, grabbing him by the shirt-front and holding him in place.

"You think?" He'd be damned if he would admit it to her, but that brief peck hadn't been what he wanted, either. His considerable restraint had, however, been in both their best interests.

"But I'm not buying it," Hannah continued as she looked deep into his eyes.

"Too bad," Dylan said.

Hannah refused to let him extricate her fingers. "I don't care about tomorrow or the day after that or the day after that," she whispered passionately. "Don't you get that?" she demanded softly, searching his eyes. "What I care about is tonight. And you. And this. And feeling good about myself and us."

Put that way, it was all the harder to resist her attempt to seduce him. And Dylan didn't try very hard as they kissed some more. Until, that was, she put her hand on his belt. Then Dylan stopped her gallantly, his hand over top of hers. Aware she could easily regret this in the morning, he told her, "I don't want to take advantage of you." Even if she wasn't being completely upfront and truthful with him.

Hannah pushed him onto his back and rolled on top of him. "Then I'll take advantage of you!"

HANNAH WASN'T DRUNK. But pretending to be three sheets to the wind was the only way to get Dylan to stop trying to wheedle information out of her, and much as she wanted to, she couldn't tell him where she had been that day, or with whom, or why. She had made a promise of confidentiality to a dear friend that she intended to honor. One day, when it was all over, maybe she would be able to tell Dylan everything. She hoped so. She yearned for everything to turn out the way she desired. But that was still far from certain, and until it was, she had made a vow to keep private things private.

In the meantime, she would deal with what she could. And the first order of business was to do something about the newfound passion blossoming inside her.

Hannah wasn't used to wanting anyone.

But that had changed the moment Dylan had charged into her life the weekend before, exuding sex and charisma. And try as she might, she could not steer herself away from it. She had wanted him all night, from the time she arrived home and found him waiting for her.

He looked so mouthwateringly handsome in anything he wore. From the sophisticated suits he favored to the casual tropical-print shirt, loose cargo slacks and Top-Siders he had on right now. He hadn't shaved that morning, and the stubble of golden-brown beard clung to his stubborn Hart jaw, giving him a faintly piratical on-vacation look she found very appealing. Dylan on TV, polished and in command, thrilled her immensely. The less polished version was even more ruggedly attractive.

"Hannah—" As he tried to fight her off, the dimples on either side of his sensual mouth grew more pronounced.

"That's it," she teased, drawing his zipper down and sliding her hand inside. As usual he was wearing silk bikini briefs. Loving the flat, hard feel of his muscled midriff, she stroked her palm across his lower abdomen. "I love it when you say my name." She loved it when he noticed her at all. And judging from the harsh rasp of his breathing, he was definitely noticing her now.

He groaned as she worked her fingers inside the

elastic and found him, hard and hot. "Stop fighting me, Dylan," she murmured against his lips, enclosing the velvety length of him in her palm. "Stop fighting this."

Hands on her shoulders, he held her still and took a long hard look into her eyes. "You do know what you're doing now, don't you?"

Hannah grinned unrepentantly as she continued to sprawl on top of him. "That's what I've been trying to tell you." That she knew the risks, the potential rewards of getting so physically close to him. And accepted them as wholeheartedly as his fevered kisses.

Okay, her plan to compartmentalize her life the way guys did was not working out all that well thus far. She'd entered this…whatever it was…with Dylan thinking she could enjoy the brief, tempestuous fling and move on, only to discover she wanted him more than she had ever expected to want him. She could see herself needing him, something that would have been unthinkable just a few days before. And she was even possibly—gulp—falling in love with him. Which was why she had to get control of at least some part of their involvement. Even if that was only the part that was happening right now. She was tired of feeling him come near her, and then pull away, only to approach her once again, more ardently than ever. It was almost as if there was something tangible and concrete, beside the fact he was leaving as soon as he got another job, if not sooner, that was keeping him away from her, that was keeping his guard up. And it was up, never more than tonight at the sports bar when he sat there looking as if he wanted to make love to her and acting as if he felt he should keep her at arm's length.

"Which is why I want to be in the driver's seat to-night," Hannah continued with a cheekiness she could only marginally feel.

Dylan grinned, amused. "And I should let you do this because...?"

Hannah shrugged, glad to feel the mood lighten-ing between them once again. Casual fun they could both handle. "You can't always be in charge," she flirted.

The mischievous twinkle in his deep brown eyes intensified. "And why is that?" he asked her huskily, playing along wholeheartedly now.

"Because sometimes I like to call the shots," Han-nah told him seriously, as the last of the alcohol in her system was burned away by the adrenaline pump-ing through her. "And right now I want this off." Hannah finished, unbuttoning his shirt and helping him lift it over his shoulders, down his arms.

"And this." She worked similar magic on his shoes and pants.

"And this." There went his briefs. Leaving him wonderfully naked for her to see. And what a sight he was, she noticed lustily. Glowing, golden skin. Smooth muscle. Enticing tufts of golden-brown hair. Long legs. Strong arms. Nice broad shoulders and a chest that was just perfect for holding. She could sit here beside him, just looking, all night long.

As he noticed the depth of her enjoyment, his own pleasure grew, too.

"Whoa," he said as she captured the male essence of him with both her hands, sculpting, molding the hard, silky length.

He trembled with arousal as she knelt and touched him with her lips, tongue, teeth. "I'm getting a little ahead of you here."

No kidding, Hannah thought, enjoying what she was doing to him as much as he liked receiving it. Who knew she was such a woman at heart?

"Way ahead," Dylan groaned several minutes later.

"Not that far," Hannah said as her nipples beaded and ached and the damp throbbing between her legs grew. Nearly mindless with desire and as impatient to be as close to him as he was to her, she paused long enough to slip off her panties, hike up her denim skirt and climb on. Dylan murmured his pleasure, one hand splaying across her lower back to hold her in place as he entered her with one long slow stroke. Filling her completely, even as his thumb and forefinger stroked her outside, tunneling through the damp curls, to find her there. Again and again, his hand matching the slow steady rhythm of his hips.

Her eyes locked with his, Hannah rose to her knees, then slid down again. Letting him know she wanted this—wanted him—even as he set the pace. Then taking the lead again, faster, harder, moving past barriers, striving toward a single goal, seeking release, until at last unable to hold back a second longer, Hannah arched and closed around him as he too relinquished control and joined her at the edge of ecstasy and beyond.

"Damn, Hannah," Dylan sighed his contentment. He folded his arms around her and brought her close to cuddle against his chest. She lay against him, her body still quaking with the aftershocks of their lovemaking, as stunned by the wantonness she felt whenever she was around him as the depth of pleasure he gave her.

Like it or not,, Hannah realized, there was no longer any question about it. This thing with Dylan was getting way more serious than she had ever intended it to be. And the only way to deal with that, and still save face, was to borrow yet another guy-coping mechanism. And make it all as light and easy and no strings attached as she could.

"Okay, you can go home now," she teased cheerfully as she rolled off and away from him, and tugged her skirt back down over her thighs. As if this were a game they had been playing and nothing more.

Dylan looked at her, not buying her act for one red-hot second. A knowing look in his eyes, he moved over her once again. He touched her face with the warmth of his hand, cupping her chin in his palm, scoring his thumb across her lower lip, looking all the while as if he wanted nothing better than to kiss her again. "I don't think so."

Once again, Hannah pretended an insouciance she couldn't begin to feel. "Why not?" she taunted right back.

Dylan rolled onto his side and propped his head on his upraised arm. "Because I haven't seen you naked yet," he said.

Hannah wished he would quit looking at her like that, as if he wanted to devour her all over again. "Sure you have," she said, rolling onto her side, too. Glad she was only minus her panties. Because if she were as naked as he, well, suffice it to say, she wouldn't be apart from him for long. "You saw me without my clothes the last time we made love."

"But I haven't unbuttoned and unzipped and removed every barrier between us tonight."

Hannah's throat went dry at the thought of him doing all that as slowly and patiently as he seemed to want to do it. How could she keep the walls up around her heart if he kept looking at her as if he wanted her to be his woman, not just tonight, but forever?

She turned her glance away and stared up at the ceiling. "Yeah, well, I wouldn't worry about it," she said.

"Why?"

She ignored his baiting even as her heart began to race. "Because there's nothing spectacular about what's under all that cotton," Hannah said, calling on all the bluster she possessed. "What is it men say?" She looked deep into his eyes. "If you've seen one pair of breasts you've seen 'em all?"

Dylan grinned at her attempt to make light of their coupling. He was already lifting her shirt, unfastening her bra and pushing it aside. The next thing she knew, her shirt was whisked away and so was her skirt, and then he was caressing her breasts. Cupping them in his hands and fitting his lips to the tips. "How about I be the judge of that?" he said, his voice a soft, sensual rumble.

She closed her eyes in bliss, able to feel him looking at her as he kissed and caressed her with his lips and teeth and tongue. "You know—" she stopped to sigh her pleasure after a bit "—if you keep this up, you're just going to make me want you all over again."

"That is the general idea," he said as he moved even lower.

"Yes, but—" She sucked in a breath as he dipped his tongue into her navel. "Dylan. We could get used to this." And that was a problem, as far as she was concerned.

Dylan paused and slid up, until he was face-to-face with her once again. "I've got news for you, sweetheart. I already *am* used to this," he told her, his handsome face a mask of primitive need. "But that's not the only reason I've got to make love to you all over again," he confided with a rough possessiveness that thrilled her to her soul.

Aware it wasn't just her getting in too deep now— it was him, too—Hannah wreathed her arms around his broad shoulders. "What's the rest?" she asked, welcoming the hard, warm weight of him.

Dylan smiled down at her tenderly and kissed each corner of her lips in turn, before looking deep into her eyes once more. "I wasn't kissing you when you climaxed," he said seriously.

Her heart doing cartwheels in her chest, Hannah met his gaze. "That's important?"

Dylan smiled at her so tenderly she was tempted to weep. "You tell me," he said, and fused their lips together once more. His mouth slanted across hers in a fierce burning kiss that encouraged her to answer his ardor with her own. Their tongues mated in an erotic dance unlike anything she had ever experienced. New sensations spiraled and ricocheted inside her. And there was nothing soft or gentle about the way they came together then. It was all so hot and fast and wild and exultant. And during it all, Dylan never stopped kissing her, never stopped claiming her as his, not even as triumph rose in their throats and she trembled and clenched around him. All was lost and then discovered in the reckless joining that defined their relationship.

DYLAN SPENT THE NIGHT forgetting his doubts and making fierce, amazing love to Hannah. But when morning came, and he awoke with Hannah sleeping sweetly beside him, reality came crashing back again.

What was he doing? he wondered as he slipped soundlessly from the bed. Getting so completely involved with a woman he wasn't sure, even now, he could completely trust? Yes, he cared about her. He might even be falling in love with her. But you couldn't love someone without trust, and there were far too many odd things about her recent behavior for him to feel anything but uneasy about the prospect of committing his heart to her.

What was it they said about guys with a romantic history like his? Once burned, twice shy. That was him, all right. And right now he was very wary of being made a fool of all over again, this time in front of family and friends, and everyone else he had grown up knowing.

Aware of all the questions he had yet to be answered, with or without Hannah's cooperation, he pulled on his briefs and slacks, and went downstairs to make coffee for them both.

Seeing her keys still lying on the counter, he went to slip them into her purse, and that was when he saw two airline boarding passes.

A quick perusal told him Hannah had been to Wilmington and back the previous day, with a three-hour layover between flights.

Why would she have gone to a coastal city one hundred and twenty miles away for just three hours? Dylan wondered. Why wouldn't she have mentioned it?

Had she gone to Wilmington alone? Of her own volition? Or at someone else's request? Dylan wondered restively. Could it be someone also connected to his equally private brother Cal? Was this part of her attempt to compartmentalize her life that she had told him about, and if so, where did he fit into the scheme of things?

THE FIRST THING HANNAH noted when she woke was the silence. The second, the coldness of the sheets beside her. She rose, aware her head was pounding, as much from lack of sleep and not enough water the previous day as the three glasses of beer she'd imbibed the night before.

She shrugged on her light cotton summer robe and went into the bathroom, brushed her teeth and washed her face. Still dragging a comb through her hair, she went down the loft stairs. The rest of the house was equally deserted. In fact, if not for the tell-tale soreness of her body, she might have thought she had dreamed the wild night of passion.

But it had been real, all right.

And so were Dylan's suspicions.

Which meant she was going to have to get this situation with Cal resolved, and soon. Or she could kiss any sort of future relationship with his younger brother Dylan goodbye.

"I KNOW HE WAS IN surgery all afternoon," Dylan chatted up Cal's secretary later that morning as he embarked on his fishing expedition at the medical center annex, where physician offices were located.

Cal's secretary, a motherly woman in her late fifties, shook her head. "No, yesterday he was off, and—"

"Is that his regular afternoon off?" Dylan interrupted.

"No. He just needed to go to Wilmington for some reason," the secretary said with a baffled smile.

"Right," Dylan nodded as if he knew all about that.

"It was the day before he was in surgery all afternoon," Cal's secretary continued affably. "Which is exactly where he's going to be all this morning, too." She regarded Dylan over the rim of her bifocals. "If you want, I could have your brother paged in the OR. Or try to work you in between some of his office appointments this afternoon."

"No." Dylan waved off the offer guiltily. He felt

bad about spying on Cal and Hannah, but damn it, the two of them had left him no choice.

"It wasn't that important," Dylan continued, flashing the megawatt smile he used on TV. "I was just hoping the two of us could get together while I'm in town," he added disarmingly. "I'll have to catch up with my brother after hours."

"Lots of luck." Cal's secretary smiled. "That brother of yours works all the time."

Not all the time. Some of the time, Cal was having private meetings and lunches and trips out of town with Hannah.

Dylan didn't know where that left him.

The odd man out of an illicit love triangle? Or the man who was going to break up the illicit liaison and put his brother back on the right track? And maybe get the woman in the end, while his brother went back to his semi-estranged wife.

The thought that Dylan could even entertain such a notion was amazing after the way he'd been burned by cheating.

And yet, there was something about Hannah, something sweet and innocent and pure at heart, that made him think if she had gotten herself involved in something unsavory it wasn't her fault. And how naive was that of him? Dylan wondered as he turned onto the street where she worked.

All Dylan knew was that he wanted—needed—to

see Hannah. So he drove down the block to her garage and found her supervising the unloading of a blue '64 Mustang convertible from the bed of a tow truck. As always, even in the blue-gray coverall she routinely wore at the garage, with her hair drawn up in a ponytail on the back of her head, she looked pretty and sexy in that wholesome small-town-girl way.

A flush appeared in her cheeks as he neared her.

Pretending for the moment the two of them hadn't made passionate love the night before, he studied the vintage sports car as if that alone was the reason he had stopped in.

"A beaut, isn't it?" Hannah asked neutrally, not quite meeting his eyes.

Dylan nodded, feeling as abruptly ill at ease as Hannah. There was so much he wanted to say to her, to ask. He didn't know where to begin. He just knew it wasn't an exchange that could be made in front of her assistant mechanic or anyone else.

So instead, he followed her lead and concentrated on the vehicle. The car looked to be in perfect condition, from the white retractable top to the mag wheels. "It looks terrific," he said. "Got a thing for '64 Mustangs?"

Hannah shrugged, the evasive light back in her emerald eyes. "Some of my customers do. What are you doing here, anyway?"

I can't stay away from you. "Want to go out this evening?" he asked.

She frowned. "Can't. I've got a chauffeur's gig tonight."

Disappointment swept through him. "Wedding?"

Again, she shook her head. "Some hotshot CEO of a California medical-research company is flying in at five this evening. He's hired me—and the Bentley—for the full night."

Dylan tried not to think what that might entail, or how Hannah might dress for the occasion. "How did he know to call you?" Dylan asked casually.

"Someone at the med center recommended me, I think," she said vaguely. "Why?"

It was Dylan's turn to shrug. "I just wondered if your reputation as a driver stretched all the way to California."

Hannah scoffed as if that was the silliest thing she had ever heard. "Don't we wish that were the case," she said wryly. She surveyed him up and down, a faintly sympathetic look coming into her eyes as she easily intuited his mood. "Don't look so glum," she told him cheerfully. "You'll find something to do in my absence."

Dylan brightened as his next thought occurred. "I could ride along with you," he said.

Hannah swiftly shook her head. "Not while I'm working."

Despite her grim certainty, some lingering hope remained. "You sure?" Dylan asked with a persuasive smile. "I could provide extra security. Carry his bags."

To his disappointment, Hannah wasn't budging. She folded her arms in front of him, her posture unyielding. "Somehow I don't think he'd go for that. And I know I don't," she added when he would have argued with her some more. She looked at him sternly. "I can do this, Dylan. I do it all the time."

He knew that. He wanted to protect her from harm anyway. "It's not that I don't believe in your driving and hauling abilities, Hannah."

Hannah propped her hands on her hips. "Then what is it exactly that bothers you about me working tonight?"

The fact you'll be with another man, doing God knows what for an entire evening. The fact that deep down I trust you not to do anything unsavory, when all the evidence says I shouldn't.

Hannah looked at him, still waiting for his explanation.

"We've got so little time to socialize together," Dylan said finally, knowing that much at least was true, even if it wasn't the whole story.

"Which is maybe why we shouldn't get too used to hanging out together in the first place, especially in the evenings," Hannah murmured testily as a familiar red '64 Mustang convertible turned in to the garage lot.

Dylan was not pleased to see R. G. Yarborough behind the wheel. Hannah, on the other hand, looked delighted as she walked over to greet the wealthy married man.

He couldn't help it. Jealousy swept through Dylan.

Slim Kerstetter sidled up to Dylan and elbowed him in the side. "Don't like that guy much, do you?" Slim observed.

Dylan frowned, annoyed to find he was wearing his heart on his sleeve where the mysterious Hannah Reid was concerned. He glanced at Slim. "Is it that obvious?"

Slim chuckled with the wisdom of his sixty-some years. "Only to anyone looking at your face. Not that I blame you." Slim turned his attention back to the wealthy customer. "I don't like him, either."

Dylan glanced at Slim, wondering how much of the goings-on Slim knew about. "Is Yarborough a steady customer?"

Slim shrugged. "Hasn't been until this week."

A fact that tied in to all his worst suspicions.

Dylan looked back over at Hannah and R. G. Yarborough.

"The thing is, I was hoping you could give me an estimate on what it would take to bring it up to top form," R.G. was saying as Dylan walked closer to where they stood in the guise of getting himself a soda from the machine, when all he really wanted to do was get close enough to hear everything the two were saying instead of just bits and pieces.

Hannah shook her head definitively. "I have to tell you, R.G. After having driven the car, it would take thousands of dollars in parts and labor to get it up to the speed of that '64 Mustang convertible over there." She pointed to the one parked on the other side of the lot.

R. G. Yarborough leaned in closer to Hannah. "I could make it worth your while," he said in a low, seductive voice. He reached out to touch her arm.

"That does it," Dylan muttered furiously, shoving his unopened soft drink at Slim. He charged forward and plucked Yarborough's hand off Hannah's arm.

"What the—?" R.G. sputtered, turning to Dylan.

"Hands off her," Dylan commanded, ready to do whatever needed to be done to make it happen.

Hannah blinked. She hadn't looked happy to have R.G. touching her. She looked even less pleased to have Dylan intervening in her behalf. "Excuse me?" She spoke as if she were the one in control.

"I don't like him touching you." Dylan glared at R. G. Yarborough, his warning clear. "So don't."

It was Yarborough's turn to look incensed. "Listen you!" R.G. grabbed a fistful of Dylan's shirt and tugged him near.

Dylan had spent his entire life on the sidelines, watching others mix it up. On the field and off. No more. "Listen yourself," Dylan shoved R. G. Yarborough right back.

The next thing Dylan knew, Hannah had ducked beneath both their outstretched arms and was standing between them. "Break it up. Right now!" she demanded, grabbing Dylan's arms. "Both of you!"

Temper simmering, Dylan stayed where he was. So did R. G. Yarborough.

"You heard the lady," another male voice said with even greater authority.

Everyone turned to look as Cal Hart strode across the parking lot toward them.

"NOT VERY SMART, intervening in her work like that," Cal told Dylan as Hannah concluded her conversation with R. G. Yarborough on the other side of the garage property, while Cal escorted Dylan in the other direction to chill out.

"What are you saying?" Dylan glared at his older brother, more sure than ever that something mysterious was going on between Cal and Hannah. Otherwise, why would Cal care if Dylan got in the first fistfight of his life and made a fool of himself over the pretty mechanic? It was Dylan's pride at stake here. Not Cal's. And if Cal was so darned busy, why was he taking time to come over and see Hannah in the middle of the day, anyway?

"I'm telling you that you should mind your own

business," Cal concluded. "And let Hannah deal with the guy in her own way." Apparently realizing Dylan was unconvinced, Cal added meaningfully, "She can defend herself."

Dylan didn't doubt that.

"The point is, she shouldn't have to," he groused.

"She knows what she's doing," Cal repeated firmly. He looked Dylan in the eye. "She's not the tomboy you remember. She's a grown woman now."

Cal had *that* right. Dylan couldn't believe he'd ever thought Hannah was ordinary looking. Lately, she'd been doing a real lousy job of hiding her femininity from the world.

However, Dylan had been hoping—irrationally, he knew—no other man had noticed. At least, not the way he had. "Meaning?"

Cal shrugged. "This isn't the first time someone's hit on her without an invitation. And, given the way she looks, little brother, it's not likely to be the last."

"You think she's attractive?" Dylan tested out Cal's feelings.

"Well, duh. Of course. I just didn't think *you* had noticed." Cal sized up Dylan in a way that made Dylan uncomfortable, as if he intuitively knew Dylan had already taken Hannah to bed. "I guess you have."

No kidding, Dylan thought, aware Cal did not sound the least bit possessive about his relationship with Hannah, whatever it was.

Hannah returned, her expression polite but firm. "Slim, Mr. Yarborough is going to leave his Mustang here to be worked on and he needs a ride back to his place."

Slim put down his wrench and wiped his hands on a rag. "No problem. I'll take him right now."

Hannah looked at Dylan. "Don't you have someplace else to be?" she asked, looking exasperated with him, but not necessarily angry at the way he had just made a fool of himself and gone all gallant on her.

Doing his best to get control of his skyrocketing emotions, Dylan shrugged in reply, and turned to look at Cal. Did he have a reason for being here? Was it a coincidence R. G. Yarborough and Cal were here at the same time? Or was there something else going on?

The only thing Dylan knew for sure, as Cal went on to schedule the forty-thousand-mile maintenance on his SUV with Hannah, was that Dylan didn't like the tangle of emotions inside him any more than he liked the doubts he was having about the woman who was fast becoming a very important part of his life.

"THANKS FOR COMING to the rescue tonight, honey," Helen Hart said later that evening.

"No problem." Dylan looked at his mom. "You know I could deejay a wedding in my sleep." He had done so many of them during his college years. It was how he had put himself through school. It had been no problem to come in at the last minute, when the other guy got sick.

"I thought maybe you could use the money, under the circumstances," Helen said gently, then forged on with difficulty. "I don't know how things are for you financially, but if you need assistance…"

Dylan did his best to curtail his irritation at the offer. He knew his mother hadn't meant to dent his pride. "I've got enough in my savings to cover it, Mom." He had always lived below his means to avoid just this conversation, in the event he ever did get fired from a TV job.

"I'm glad to hear that," Helen murmured.

Across the crowded ballroom, Dylan saw Hannah walk in. She was still in her chauffeur's uniform and headed for the corridor that led to the kitchen.

Wondering if she was still irked at him for coming to her defense earlier, he stayed to announce the next two songs, then set the stereo for back-to-back play and walked to the kitchen.

Hannah was sitting in a chair, looking as pretty and relaxed as ever. The inn's head chef, Vonda Gilbert, was putting a plate in front of her. She grinned over at him, looking incredibly happy considering the long day she had put in, first at the garage, and then behind the wheel of her Bentley. He found himself wondering what was up.

"Hey, Dylan."

"Hey yourself." Giving in to impulse, he touched her shoulder briefly, then sat down at the table, glad to see she was apparently no longer irritated with him for coming to her aid. Either that, or she was so embarrassed by his behavior she had decided their mutual dignity was better served if they simply pretended the incident hadn't happened. Dylan was okay with that. Whenever hideously embarrassed, he preferred to just move on. "So how'd your gig go?" Dylan asked, shaking off his brooding mood and matching her outward cheer.

In answer, Hannah flushed and reached into her shirt. She pulled a wad of hundred-dollar bills out of her bra. "See for yourself."

Dylan took the money and blinked, stunned as he examined the money still warmed from her skin. "How much is that?" he asked, handing it back.

Hannah leaned closer and whispered as happily as a kid who had just earned her first A in school. "Two thousand dollars! Can you believe it?" She practically trembled with excitement. "Just for one evening's work!"

Dylan struggled not to conclude the obvious. He cleared his throat, continued hoarsely, "What should he have paid you?"

"For driving?" Still grinning merrily, Hannah paused to pop a grape in her mouth. "Around four hundred. But hey, if he wants to show his largesse by giving me an incredible tip, that's fine with me. So—" she eyed Dylan, obviously in the mood for celebrating her good fortune "—you about done here?"

Dylan nodded, listening to the music in the background, calculating how much time he had left. "I just have to say good night to everyone at the end of this song." The bride and groom had already left for their honeymoon. Only a few stragglers remained at the reception.

Mischief gleamed in Hannah's eyes, making her look—once again—like one of the guys. "Want to head over to Mac's with me?" She glanced at her watch, oblivious to the fact it wasn't quite the invitation he had hoped to receive. "The Thursday-night poker game should be starting soon."

THERE WERE FOUR OTHER guys in addition to Hannah, Dylan and Mac. Cal came in after midnight. He'd been in surgery all evening, but, like everyone else except Hannah, did not have to be at work early the next day.

"Sandwiches, beer and chips are in the kitchen," Mac directed.

"Thanks." Cal headed off as Mac tossed everyone a pack of the colored chips that would be used for betting.

Hannah rose. "I'll see if he needs anything." She exited the living room and headed down the hall that led to the rear of the house.

"Since when did she start waiting on any of us?" Tim Harmon asked.

Dylan rose, his manner casual. "I'm going to get another sandwich. Anyone want anything?"

The guys shook their heads as Mac shuffled the deck and dealt cards all around. As Dylan neared the kitchen, he heard Hannah say, "It worked exactly like we predicted. He's already starting to talk a trade with me."

A trade of what? Dylan wondered suspiciously, peering around the corner to see Hannah and Cal standing close together.

"Is he being reasonable?" Cal asked as he loaded his plate.

"Of course not." Hannah scoffed, opening a beer for him. Dylan's gut knotted up even more. "You know how rich people are. They always want something for a whole lot of nothing. But you give me a little time and I'm sure I'll get you what you want. No question."

"Thanks, Hannah. In the meantime, though—" Cal released a weary breath "—I'm just afraid if Ashley finds out what you and I've been doing, she'll take it as a sign that she and I shouldn't be together."

No kidding! Dylan's heart went out to his sister-in-law, who probably had no idea what was going on back here in North Carolina while she was over in Honolulu, finishing her fellowship.

"I promise I won't tell a soul," Hannah soothed.

Cal nodded at Hannah, in what Dylan could only suppose was gratitude, then started to turn toward Dylan.

Hurriedly, Dylan moved back, out of sight, then started forward again with enough momentum that he and Cal practically crashed into each other as Cal came out the door. Pretending he hadn't heard or seen a thing, Dylan smiled at them both. "Any more beer in here?" Dylan asked cheerfully.

Hannah smiled at him and picked up the bowl of chips.

As their eyes met, Hannah blushed a little. Whether out of guilt or embarrassment at having been nearly caught in a tête-à-tête with Dylan's married brother, Dylan didn't know. And he wasn't sure that he wanted to know.

Chapter Eight

"Want to come in?" Hannah said when Dylan parked at the curb in front of her house.

"I don't think I'd better," Dylan said truthfully. He had a lot to sort out and none of it needed to be done between the sheets. "It's awfully late."

Briefly, hurt flashed across Hannah's face. She opened the car door, and the vehicle's interior lights came on. The added illumination made her appear even more vulnerable, before the emotion in her eyes receded once again. "Sure. I understand," she said.

Although, Dylan noted, clearly she did not. She wanted him to come in. And possibly, make love to her again. And truth be told, there was nothing he would rather be doing. If only he could trust her as much as he needed to. "I'll see you tomorrow?" Dylan said, hoping to soften the blow of what she obviously saw as his rejection. "That is, if it's still okay for me to use your computer while you're at work."

Hannah nodded stiffly. "It's fine."

She got out of the car and moved gracefully up the walk, toward the front door. Dylan waited until she was safely inside, then, still struggling with the guilt he felt over hurting her feelings, he drove back to Mac's house. The lights upstairs were already out, signaling Mac had probably gone to bed as soon as all the poker buddies had left. Happy to have the privacy he needed, Dylan cut the engine on his rental car and whipped out his cell phone. He scrolled through the list of numbers in the address book and then punched the one for Cal's wife's cell phone. "I'm not sure what the time difference is between North Carolina and Honolulu," Dylan told Ashley as soon as they had connected.

"Since you're on daylight saving time right now, it is six hours," Ashley replied. "Which makes it 8:00 p.m. here, but two in the morning there. So what's up? Cal is all right, isn't he?" Familial concern laced her low voice.

That was what Dylan was trying to find out. "Cal's fine," Dylan said. At least from a health perspective anyway. "I was just wondering how you are," Dylan said casually.

"What do you mean?"

"Well," Dylan hedged, not sure how to broach such a tricky subject. "You missed Janey and Thad's wedding…"

"Because I couldn't get the time off from my fellowship," Ashley said. She paused briefly and suspicion crept into her voice. "Didn't Cal tell you?"

"Yes."

"But you're not buying it," Ashley deduced sagely.

"Well, it has been a while since anyone in the family has seen you," Dylan said. *Over a year and a half to be exact.*

"I thought you understood how difficult it was for me to make a twelve-hour flight back to North Carolina," Ashley said. "Not counting the time change. Since I've been out here, it's just been easier for Cal and I to fly an equal distance and meet up on the West Coast."

It wasn't lost on Dylan or anyone else that Ashley had been ducking the rest of the Hart family, too. Cal had said she wasn't seeing much of her own parents, either.

"Was Cal upset with me about missing Janey and Thad's wedding?" Ashley continued warily.

"He said he understood."

"But you don't believe it," Ashley guessed.

"I'm just wondering if things are okay with you two," Dylan said kindly.

Ashley sighed. A long silence followed. "I'm not sure I should talk to you about this."

Dylan cringed, aware he was being obtrusive to the point of rudeness, but seeing no other way. "I'm trying to help you both," he said. "Because I love you both."

"I realize that."

"But you don't think I can?"

Another lengthy pause. "Dylan, I know you mean well, but I just can't talk to you about this! And I don't think you should question Cal, either!" Ashley said a hurried goodbye and hung up.

Dylan sat looking at the cell phone in his hand, aware all he had managed to confirm was that Cal and Ashley weren't communicating very well. The question was why? What did Hannah have to do with Cal's marital troubles? Was she, or whatever they were both up to, a distraction? Had Cal lost his way in more than one area? Had Ashley sensed that? And become troubled and resentful? Were money problems the root of Cal and Ashley's strife, too? Were Cal and Hannah drawn together in some sort of con to get quick cash that would solve both their problems? That made sense. Sort of. Although Dylan had always thought both Cal and Hannah had more character than that. On the other hand, desperate people did desperate things. The question was, how desperate were Cal and Hannah?

The only thing Dylan knew for sure was that he wouldn't have all the answers about that tonight. Which left one problem to pursue—his current employment. Deciding to check his messages to see if anything had developed on that front, he dialed in. He was just getting the last message off his home answering machine when the front door opened and Mac, clad only in a pair of jeans, came striding out.

"What are you doing?" Mac got straight to the point. "I heard you drive up fifteen minutes ago."

"Just checking my messages," Dylan said truthfully.

Mac's eyebrow arched. "Must have been mighty interesting," he said.

Dylan shrugged, and knowing he had to tell his eldest brother something, related, with no small degree of pride, "Apparently, viewers at my former TV station in Chicago have started a campaign to bring me back. Thus far the station has received over six hundred requests I be reinstated."

Mac grinned. "That *is* pretty impressive."

Dylan nodded.

"Think it'll work?"

"No clue," Dylan said. "It's always possible. Anything's possible."

"Then the question is," Mac said slowly as Dylan got out of the car, "do you want to go back?"

MAC'S QUESTION WAS a good one, and it was still haunting Dylan the next day when he went over to the garage to see if Hannah wanted to have lunch with him, only to discover she wasn't there. "Went to look at samples at Countertops Galore in Raleigh," Slim said.

Dylan frowned. Both the garage minivan and the Bentley were in the lot. "What'd she drive? Her vehicles are both here."

"Aren't you the nosy one," Slim teased. He bent back over the Lexus engine he was working on. "If you must know, she took that blue Mustang."

She'd certainly had a lot of contact in '64 Mustang convertibles recently. He didn't recall her ever being a Mustang enthusiast, before now, anyway. Although Cal had liked them a lot for a while when he was in college, Dylan seemed to recall. But he'd never owned one, and neither had Ashley. "Why did she drive that?" Dylan asked.

"Said she wanted to test-drive it," Slim explained, a mixture of curiosity and exasperation on his weather-beaten face. "And given the fact she owns this garage, and I work for her, I didn't question her on that."

If only he could be so…disinterested…in Hannah's doings, Dylan thought.

Still debating whether or not to check up on Hannah's whereabouts to see if she really was where she'd said she would be, Dylan dropped by his sister's house. Janey and Thad had come back from their brief honeymoon the previous evening, and his mother had asked him to bring them a few wedding presents that had arrived while they were gone.

The thirty-three-year-old Janey was dressed in capri pants and a pastel T-shirt, instead of the white chef's apron she usually wore in her bakery. Her straight and silky chestnut hair fell in loose waves to her shoulders. The blush of vacation sun was on her pretty face. Her amber eyes glowed with an inner contentment Dylan envied.

Her six-foot-four husband, Thad Lantz, looked equally tan and fit and rested as he shook Dylan's hand.

"Thanks," Janey said, accepting the gifts.

Dylan couldn't help but note his sister looked a lot better than he had, returning from his own honeymoon, several years before. In fact, she looked happier than he had ever seen her. Which just showed you the effect real love could have on your life. They chitchatted briefly, then Dylan got down to what was on his mind.

"What do you know about the trouble in Cal and Ashley's marriage?" he asked.

"Very little," Janey said. "I didn't think I should go nosing around in their private business."

"I agree with Janey," Thad said, the ends of his dark mustache slanting downward. "Whatever Cal and Ashley's problems, it really isn't any of our concern."

"But if their marriage is truly on the rocks. If we could do something—anything—to help," Dylan said.

Thad shoved a hand through his dark curly hair. "Look, I know we haven't been brothers-in-law for long, but I am seriously advising you to stay out of whatever is going on between your brother and his wife. A third party inserted into a marriage already suffering some difficulty can speed it to an end faster than you can skate from one end of the ice to the other."

Knowing Thad, Dylan had half expected a hockey metaphor from the Carolina Storm coach. Dylan knew Thad was also speaking from experience, since Thad and his previous wife had divorced after she became involved with another man, whom she had later married.

"What are you getting at, Dylan?" Janey frowned as she put a glass of iced tea with lemon in front of him. "Do you think it's really that bad? Are Cal and Ashley headed for a divorce? I mean, I was hoping it was just the physical separation from each other causing the tension between them and that once she was finished with her fellowship and they were living together again, they'd be happy!"

Dylan had hoped so, too, but after talking to Ashley the night before, Dylan felt the situation was more dire than anyone in the family wanted to admit. Ashley had never been one to confide in any of her in-laws, true. But Dylan felt sure that had it just been loneliness that was the problem, that Ashley would have said something to that effect. If only to stop his questions, put his mind at ease. She hadn't. Instead, she had hesitated. Gotten defensive, edgy and tried to keep him from putting the very same questions to Cal. So what was going on that Ashley didn't want him or anyone else in the family to know? What was driving the two apart? Was there a third party involved in Cal and Ashley's marriage? And was that person the woman he was fast falling in love with?

"SINCE WHEN DID YOU become interested in manual labor?" Cal asked Dylan from the front door of Hannah's home later that same afternoon.

Dylan wiped the sweat from his face. "Since it became clear to me the only way Hannah would get her cabinets completely installed this afternoon was if I lent a hand."

And because maybe if her house were finished and she didn't have money problems, Hannah would stop whatever it was she was up to with Cal and turn all her attention to him. And then he could let the past be the past and just concentrate on his future with Hannah. And he did, Dylan realized, want a future with Hannah, even if all that future could include—for the present anyway—was a long-distance romance.

"What's it to you, anyway?" Dylan challenged. Why should Cal be nosing around in Hannah's relationship with him?

"Nothing." Cal walked in as if invited. "And everything." Cal looked around at the three men busy fitting the cabinets into place. "Is there someplace we can talk privately?"

Dylan grabbed a bottle of water from the cooler on the floor and led Cal to the backyard.

"Ashley called me this morning," Cal said.

Hellfire and damnation.

"She said you had been nosing around in our affairs."

Dylan decided not to deny it. "So?"

"So neither of us asked you to play marriage counselor."

"I didn't mean to pry."

"But?" Cal prodded.

"I know unhappiness when I see it." Dylan drank deeply, then wiped his mouth with the back of his hand. "I know when all the pieces of a picture aren't quite adding up. And I know what it's like to want to stay in a state of denial so you won't have to admit to yourself how screwed up your love life really is."

Cal's shoulders relaxed ever so slightly as he watched Dylan take another long, thirsty drink. "What would you know about a love life?" He scowled. "I don't recall you ever being seriously involved with anyone for any length of time."

Guilt flooded Dylan as he thought about all he had kept from his family, allegedly because he wanted to protect them, when deep down he knew it was really for the sake of his pride. Because he hadn't wanted them or anyone else to know how seriously he had flubbed up in ever getting involved with a schemer like Desirée in the first place.

"You and I both know there is something very wrong with your marriage. Hell, everybody knows it. Everybody also knows you and Ashley were as deeply in love with each other as it was possible for two people to be in the beginning."

"That was twelve years ago." Cal shoved a hand through his hair.

"Right. And you two have a decade-long relationship and two and a half years of marriage to show for it." Dylan put the cap back on his water bottle. "So don't let whatever it is that is going on with you right now mess that up."

HANNAH WALKED INTO HER house at seven-thirty that evening, stunned to see two things. First, her entire set of kitchen cabinets had been hung. And two, the sneaker and shorts-clad Dylan, who was in the process of handing out tickets and saying goodbye to the crew, appeared to have had a very active part in what had been going on.

"Nice work, guys." Hannah smiled at Dylan and the three installers, appreciating how much work had gone into hanging the white bead-board cabinets just so. There were no countertops yet—just pieces of plywood fit temporarily over the tops—and the kitchen sink still needed to be put in, too. But she could see how terrific the kitchen was all going to look when it was finished, and that was really exciting. It made her feel as if all the inconvenience she had endured during the two-year renovation was going to be worth it.

Dylan waited until the men had left, then turned to Hannah. He had taken off his shirt and looked incredibly handsome and at ease. Not that she planned to let it affect her, in any case. Hannah had realized last night, when Dylan declined to come in after the poker game, that she had been wearing her heart on her sleeve where he was concerned. No more. From now on she was going to play it cool. As for tonight, well, it was too bad he was here. She had been hoping he would have already left by the time she arrived. Since he hadn't, she would just have to show him how immune she was to him.

"This how you wanted the cupboards arranged?" he asked her, looking pretty proud of himself.

She flashed him an efficient smile, the kind she usually reserved for auto-shop customers. "Yes."

He glanced at the placard in her hand. "Are those the countertop samples?"

Again, Hannah nodded. Why wouldn't he just leave? Why did he suddenly look as if he wanted to be very good friends with her again…more than friends?

Dylan edged closer as he slipped his short-sleeved tropical-print sport shirt back on. "Know which one of those you want?" he asked nonchalantly.

Hannah nodded. "The black marble, but the salesman wanted me to bring the sample home and hold it up against the walls and the floor and look at it in both artificial light and daylight, to make absolutely sure, before I made a final decision."

"How long before it comes in?" Dylan buttoned his shirt from midsternum down.

Hannah headed up the stairs to the loft, dismayed to find Dylan following her. "Approximately a month after I order it, but I can't do that until I have the seven thousand."

Dylan stopped in front of the desk in her bedroom and exited the e-mail program before turning off her computer. "When will that be?" he asked casually.

Hannah crossed to her bureau and took out a pair of shorts and a T-shirt. She disappeared into the bathroom and shut the door behind her. "That all depends on how many moonlighting jobs I get," she called out. Sad to say, most did not pay as well as her chauffeuring job the evening before.

Dylan spoke to her through the closed door. "Have you eaten dinner yet?"

"Nope." Trying not to admit what his low sexy voice was doing to her, Hannah tugged off the jeans and long-sleeved shirt she'd worn to work and put on the shorts and T-shirt.

"Are you hungry?" Dylan asked hopefully.

"Not really." Hannah tugged a brush through her hair and pulled her auburn hair up into a ponytail on the back of her head.

"What do you have planned for this evening?"

Dylan asked as Hannah tossed her dirty clothes into the hamper and emerged from the bathroom.

She looked at Dylan, and, pausing only to slip her bare feet into a pair of bright orange flip-flops, answered drolly.

"What's with the third degree?"

He merely shrugged, raising an eyebrow expectantly.

Clearly, he wasn't going to back off until he accounted for every moment of her evening.

"What else? More work."

"What kind of work?" Dylan pressed, as he followed her back downstairs.

Hannah focused grimly on the chore ahead as she headed into the garage to get the cleaning supplies she needed. "I'm going to wash the Bentley."

DYLAN KNEW IF HE WERE any sort of gentleman he would have taken one of Hannah's many not-so-subtle hints and left her in peace for the evening. He decided he was no gentleman, because being a gentleman was not going to win Hannah's heart. The only way he'd get her devotion was if he took a page from his hockey-playing brother-in-law's book and charged full speed ahead toward his goal.

"This must be worth a pretty penny," Dylan said picking up a sponge and soaping down the other side of the Bentley. He was beginning to know how his brothers Joe and Fletcher must have felt when they went all out to pursue the ladies in their lives.

"More than the house—prerenovation, anyway," she replied, just as casually. She continued to watch him cautiously, as if wondering what he was up to now.

"How long has the car been in your family?" Dylan recalled the British luxury car from when he was a kid. It was the only one in town, and the sleek white four-door sedan with the sleekly curved top and majestic front grill attracted attention wherever it went.

"My grandfather inherited it from a grateful customer when I was ten," Hannah said. "He drove it occasionally, but mostly it just sat in the garage."

"Until you turned it into a limo."

Hannah tossed him a wry smile. "I had to do something to be able to pay for the insurance on it. And I must admit, I love driving it."

She looked good behind the wheel, too. Like she belonged there.

He watched as Hannah knelt to scrub out a wheel rim. "You really don't have to stay and help me do this," she said again.

You're not going to get rid of me that easily, Dylan thought. Although why he was suddenly so prone to getting emotionally and physically involved with a woman he couldn't completely trust, he couldn't say. All he knew for sure was that Hannah was headed for trouble, and he couldn't just walk away and let her destroy her life. Or anyone else's. And that being the case, he had a test to give. He picked up the garden hose. "I talked to Cal today," Dylan said nonchalantly as he rinsed the place he had just cleaned. "He and Ashley are having problems."

Shoulders tensed, Hannah kept her eyes averted. "Cal tell you that?" she asked matter-of-factly.

Dylan frowned, hoping that wasn't guilt he saw on her face. "Not exactly."

Still not looking at him, Hannah went back to methodically washing her side of the Bentley. "Maybe you should stay out of it," she advised.

Exactly what Cal, Janey and Thad had said. Although none of them had evidenced any difficulty looking him in the eye while the matter was discussed. "I want my brother's marriage to survive," Dylan stated quietly.

Hannah sobered and abruptly looked as worried as Dylan felt. She gazed up at him. "I think everyone does," she told Dylan in a low empathetic voice.

So if that was the case, what was Hannah doing keeping secrets with Cal? Was whatever they were meeting about somehow connected with Ashley? Or had Hannah simply convinced herself, just as Dylan's ex had, that what she did with one man was no one else's business—even if that man was married? Was *whatever* this was with Cal Hannah's attempt to compartmentalize her life?

He recalled something Hannah had told him the night of the benefit, about the way she felt post Rupert Wallace. *It made me want to never be truly vulnerable or involved with anyone again… It made me want to compartmentalize my life the way guys do, and put sex here, and fun here and no commitment ever over here…*

Perhaps that was what was going on here, Dylan mused. If so, which category did he fall into? Sex? Fun? No commitment ever?

"I also think we should not be talking about them or their problems," Hannah continued scolding.

Aware she had never been prone to gossip, any more than he was, Dylan nodded in agreement.

"So how was your day?" Hannah asked, changing the subject.

"A lot better than I expected. I got a job offer in Chicago."

Hannah looked happy for him. "From your old station?"

Dylan shook his head, and tried not to notice how long and shapely Hannah's legs looked in the trim-fitting khaki shorts. Or how well her breasts filled out the soft white T-shirt. "No, although there's a campaign to reinstate me. The offer came from a rival. Which also happens to be the number-one local station in that market. And they've offered me ten percent more in salary."

Hannah paused, disappointment flashing briefly in her pretty, emerald eyes. Collecting herself, she smiled enthusiastically. "When do you leave?"

Dylan shrugged, wishing she weren't being so good about this. It would have done more for his ego and he would have had a better idea where he stood with her, if she had behaved as if she was going to miss him as much as he was going to miss her. But able to tell her none of that, without sacrificing what little was left of his pride, he said simply, "I've got a week to think about it."

"But you're going to accept the job," she ascertained cautiously, searching his face.

"Not necessarily," Dylan said. "I've still got an interview in San Francisco next week, a lunch and a potential offer from my old station manager here, and a chance, however slim, at the Storm announcing job." For the first time in his life, his career was less important than the person he wanted to be near. And that was astonishing, since he had been wed to his work for as long as he had worked in the broadcasting field.

"Well, sounds like you're set in any case." Hannah carefully carried the bucket and sponges through the garage to the patio behind the house.

Dylan re-coiled the hose on the reel hidden behind the bushes, at the front of the house. "I won't be unemployed if that's what you mean," he said. As always, when it came to his chosen profession, he would be fine.

Hannah slid behind the wheel and drove the Bentley into the garage.

Finished, he followed her and she hit the remote that closed the overhead garage door. Then she stalked back out to the patio, through the rear door, and over to a second garden hose—this one for the backyard.

"I'm happy things are working out for you." She dumped out the dirty water, rinsed the sponges with the hose, then filled the bucket with soapy water once again and dropped the thick pastel-colored car sponges in to soak.

Darkness was falling around them. They were standing in the wedge of artificial light streaming out from the garage. It shouldn't have necessarily been a romantic setting, but somehow, to Dylan, it was. And she realized it, too. Which was maybe why she was suddenly putting up an emotional force field once again.

"Are you?" Dylan wasn't sure why. He just knew he wanted—needed—her to tell him how she felt, instead of just muttering the expected congratulations. Maybe if they could talk about the job opportunities facing him, openly and honestly, they could acknowledge their feelings about each other…and everything else standing between them. Because, if she would just open up to him, he would go after her, no holds barred. And he wouldn't stop until he had won her heart, forever.

Oblivious to the ardent direction of his thoughts, she stared at him a long moment. "Dylan, please. Don't push this. Don't push me," she said quietly as she bent over to pick up a sponge out of the water and wrung it out.

He watched as she picked up the second sponge. "Why not?" Why shouldn't they push it? Why shouldn't they fight—if that's what they were about to do—every bit as passionately and unreservedly as they had made love to each other? Why shouldn't they both just go for it—for each other—the same way they both went after everything and anything else they wanted in this life?

She looked him up and down, her patience clearly at an end. Color swept into her high, sculpted cheeks. "Because you've already done much too much of *that* as it is, that's why."

He closed the distance between them, aware that the time for holding back was at an end. "You're mad at me."

She rolled her eyes and kept him at bay with the dripping sudsy sponge in her upraised palm. "Brilliant deduction there, TV Man."

Dylan took her in his arms, anyway. "Why?"

"Oh, I don't know." Temper flaring visibly now, Hannah shoved him in the chest with the wet, soapy sponge, dampening them both. "Maybe it has something to do with the fact you make love to me one night—" she shoved him again, for emphasis "—and get all territorial over me in front of a customer the next day. And then, after the poker game, *can't even be bothered to get out of the car and walk me to my front door.*"

So, Dylan thought triumphantly, she had missed being with him as much as he had missed being with her the previous evening. Now they were getting somewhere.

Deciding both of them were sudsy enough, he took the sponge from her hand and ever so deliberately dropped it back into the bucket. Ignoring the way the wet fabric molded the soft curves of her breasts, delineating soft mounds and jutting nipples, he leaned in closer and asked her point-blank. "Did you want me to walk you to your door last night? Did you want me to kiss you senseless and come in and make wild, passionate love to you all over again?"

She folded her arms in front of her and glared at him. "Not anymore I don't."

He smiled, knowing when a lady protested far too much. "Oh, really," he drawled, eyeing her softly parted lips.

"Yes, really," Hannah repeated, emerald eyes flashing hotly.

"Then prove it," Dylan dared in a low, silky voice.

Breath coming raggedly, Hannah tossed her head and pivoted on her heel. "You prove it," she muttered, walking away.

Chapter Nine

Hannah made it as far as the flowers edging the patio when she got hit in the back with a wet, soapy sponge. She turned and saw the mischief shimmering in Dylan's eyes. "I can't believe you just did that," she said.

"Yeah?" He bent and picked up the back yard hose and squirted her on the knee. "Then believe this."

"You're being childish," Hannah said.

"Am I?" He squirted her other knee with a blast of sun-warmed water.

Hannah faced him, legs braced apart, and considered him lazily. "Cut it out."

Her ankle got hit with a blast of water. He chuckled as she glared at him. His glance drifted over her leg-baring khaki shorts, transparent white T-shirt and bright orange flip-flops before returning to her face. "Make me."

Hannah could see he thought she wouldn't dare to take him on.

She headed toward him slowly, wincing only slightly as he squirted her on the thigh and one arm. "I don't think so." She adopted the most bored tone she could manage as she dropped first one sponge, then the other into the soap bucket.

"Ah, come on, Hannah, play with me," he cajoled softly.

"Play with you," Hannah repeated, buying a little time.

"Yeah. Have fun? You know. Kind of like when we were kids."

"And we could do and say whatever we wanted?"

"Right."

Hannah wrung out the sponges one at a time, set them aside. Eyes serious, she looked up at Dylan, buying time. Preparing for a sneak attack. "But we're not kids anymore, Dylan," she told him sadly, picking up the bucket. "Because if we were kids I certainly wouldn't have dared do this," she continued as she grabbed the front of his shorts with one hand, tipped the bucket with the other and drenched the entire front of him.

He let out a shout and turned on the hose nozzle once again. The next thing she knew, he had grabbed the front of her shorts and turned the spray downward. She gasped as the water in the hose turned from summer warm to underground cold. Screamed again, and fought for control of the hose. He won, until she flattened her foot on his shin and tried to knock him backward. He didn't fall but he did loosen his grip on the hose just for a moment and that was all it took for her to get the nozzle and spray him in the face. He gasped and promised revenge.

The next thing Hannah knew, they were rolling in the grass, still fighting for control, both of them drenched and gasping. Then the hose was between them, still flooding them both with cool water, and his hands were on her shoulders, his lips pressed against hers. Hot. Demanding. Evoking wave after wave of blissful need, even as darkness fell around them and the ground beneath them got wetter and wetter, as did their clothes.

Finally, Dylan lifted his head. Aware she had thick hedges surrounding her backyard, but no privacy fence, he said, "Maybe we should take this inside?"

Wanting him more than she could ever recall wanting anyone or anything, knowing he wasn't going to be there much longer, Hannah nodded.

THEY MADE IT AS FAR AS the hood of the Bentley. "Not exactly the use of the vehicle I would have imagined," Hannah said as they kicked off their wet shorts, and Dylan tugged off his shirt, then hers.

"But an appropriate one, nevertheless," he said, pulling her forward and stepping into the open V of her legs. He kissed his way down her throat, to her breasts. "Given the fact this is your fantasy car."

"And fantasy is what this is," Hannah murmured while Dylan made his way to her mouth once again, kissing her long and hard and deep. She moaned and he pulled her even tighter into his arms. She felt his arousal pressing against her. His tongue stroked hers, and her middle fluttered weightlessly as his hands cupped her breasts and nimbly worked her nipples to aching crowns. He kissed her again and again, until she ached to have him and she whimpered. "I can't… wait…"

"Neither can I."

He stroked her, readying her, and then he was deep inside her. Straining against her, possessing her, letting her know he wanted her as wildly and passionately as she wanted him. Pushing herself up a little higher, she arched her back, wrapped her legs around his waist and drew him deeper still, kissing him over and over again, until she felt connected to him, not just physically, but heart and soul. And that swiftly, they were both catapulting over the edge. Shuddering, their breath rough and noisy, they clung together.

"Well," Dylan murmured eventually as he cuddled her closer in his arms. "This isn't exactly how I envisioned my first time making love in a car. Well, actually *on* a car."

"It's a first for me, too." Hannah grinned.

He kissed her temple and went all protective on her again. "Are you hungry?" he asked gently.

After that workout? "Starved."

His eyes connected with hers and held for several breath-stealing seconds. "I'd say let's go in the kitchen and whip something up," Dylan teased.

Hannah sighed, thinking of the construction mess that had been there for months. She wrinkled her nose at him. "Not quite possible, is it?"

Dylan stroked a hand through her hair. "Do you want to go out or order in?" His expression said he was amenable either way. Which was another thing she liked about him. He was adaptable where a lot of men wouldn't have been.

She smiled. "Order in."

AN HOUR LATER, they were eating the last of the kung pao chicken, pot stickers and beef and broccoli in Hannah's bed. Dylan's clothes were in the wash, along with hers.

Hannah sipped the last of her plum wine and tilted her head at Dylan. She knew this wasn't going to last. She didn't care. It was enough she'd experienced such exhilarating passion just once in her life. It had to be.

She tilted her head at him, studying his body. "You look kind of nice in just a towel." His shoulders were so broad and masculine, the muscles of his chest compact but sturdy. She found the mat of crisp golden-brown hair on his chest incredibly sexy.

Dylan's dark brown eyes glimmered with humor. "I feel at a disadvantage here, though."

"Why?" She let herself look her fill of his long, muscular legs and bare feet.

He grinned as he leaned back against the headboard. "You're dressed." His eyes roved her low-slung black knit workout pants and cropped tank top. "I'm not."

Hannah shrugged as she moved the empty white cartons from her bed to the nightstand. The fabric of her clothing moved with her, which was good because she wasn't wearing any undergarments. "Someone had to answer the door."

"True." He waved his chopsticks at her as he finished the rest of his rice.

"Without alarming the neighbors," Hannah continued stretching out opposite him so she could continue to look her fill.

He tickled the bottom of her bare foot. "Or the deliveryperson."

Hannah struggled not to giggle as she faced him with mock solemnity. "There's something to be said for not shocking everyone we know."

Dylan sighed. "I think the two of us are shocked enough."

Something in her went very still at the seriousness

of his low voice. "What do you mean?" She felt something happening here. Something huge.

Dylan put the empty carton aside and moved down to stretch out beside her so they were once again lying face-to-face. He reached out to stroke her hair. "I've never felt like this, Hannah," he told her tenderly. "About anyone."

She hadn't expected that. But now that the confession was out there… She swallowed hard around the growing knot in her throat. "I haven't felt like this, either," she admitted hoarsely.

Dylan continued sifting his fingers through her hair. "So what are we going to do about it?" he asked her.

Hannah shrugged. "I'm not sure there's much we can do," she murmured shyly.

Dylan took her free hand and kissed the back of it. "That's where you're wrong," he promised her, searching her face. "This doesn't have to be just a fling."

Didn't it? Hannah's hopes rose even as she reminded herself sternly that he was leaving. Maybe not today or tomorrow, but soon… And yet, she wanted to hear him out, foolish as it might be, given that her heart was now on the line. "What are you suggesting?" she asked him.

The conflicted look was back in his eyes. "I'm not sure."

Hannah sighed. She sat up cross-legged on the bed and let her forearms rest on her thighs. "I can't leave

Holly Springs, Dylan. My business, my home, everything I've worked so hard for is here."

"I know that." He sat up, too, mirroring her body language.

Afraid if she continued looking at him, she would give too much of her feelings away, Hannah ducked her head. She plucked at the rumpled covers. "And I'm not sure long-distance relationships work all that well," she continued.

Dylan cupped her chin in his hand and forced her gaze up to his. "They can," he said.

Hannah wanted to believe everything was going to be fine. More than fine. But the realistic side of her knew better than to count on something the odds were against. "That's what Cal and Ashley thought," Hannah reminded him. "And look what happened to them."

Dylan's glance narrowed. He studied her almost suspiciously. "What *has* happened to them, Hannah?" he asked her sternly, as if she knew something about Cal and Ashley's marriage that he didn't. Which in a roundabout way she sort of did. Fighting the guilt flowing through her, as well as the need to keep a friend's confidence, as promised, Hannah shook her head. She hadn't meant to, but she had already said far too much. "I don't want to talk about them, Dylan. Or anyone else for that matter. Especially if this is all the time we have left," she finished before he could disagree.

And to make sure they didn't, she reached over and unknotted his towel. That was all it took to get him on the same track as she. The next thing Hannah knew, he had reached over and pulled her onto his lap, kissing her with the abandon she had come to know. She reveled in the hot, insistent demand of his mouth over hers, the urgent thrust and parry of his tongue. She moaned and melted against him, her hands curling around his shoulders.

"I had a feeling this was going to happen again," she murmured as he slipped his fingers beneath the elastic bottom of her workout top and lifted the stretchy fabric over her head, baring her breasts to his view.

"Then that makes two of us," Dylan said, circling her breasts and cupping the weight with his hands. She thrilled as he bent to pay homage with his lips and tongue until her nipples were tight and achy.

She was ready for him then, but she found he was just getting started. He drew her nipple full into his mouth, suckling gently, first one, then the other. When she was nearly mindless with pleasure, he stopped to cup them both with his hands, tracing the stiff peaks with his fingertips, pausing to admire them before kissing them all over again.

Hannah moaned and rested her forehead against the back of his. "If you keep this up, it's going to take all night," she whispered.

"Exactly what I had in mind," Dylan said, drawing her back down on the bed and stretching out beside her. He looked deep into her eyes. "We don't have to hurry, Hannah. We have all night."

He certainly made her feel that way. "There's something to be said for rushing to completion," she said.

He tossed away his towel and peeled off her pants, leaving her as naked as he. "You only say that because you haven't tried this with me. Trust me. You may like fast and furious—"

"Oh, I do," Hannah said as he found her most sensitive place, then moved away.

"But you're going to like slow and easy even better."

"Dylan." She groaned when he turned her onto her stomach and began to massage his way down her spine. Touching, caressing, arousing every inch with the same deliberation he had paid her breasts. Moving lower, lower still. Putting something—the perfumed skin lotion she left on the nightstand—onto his hands and rubbing that in, too. He massaged her down her back, to her waist, the base of her spine, and lower still. Then he caressed every inch of her buttocks, the cleft between, and moved to her ankles, working his way up, so thoroughly and gently she couldn't help but moan—even as her body turned into a melting warmth of wanting.

"I'm going to pay you back for this," Hannah murmured when he finally turned her over and began working his magic on her other half.

Dylan smiled down at her, rubbing more lotion into his hands. "I'm looking forward to it," he said.

And then his hands were everywhere once again, kneading, caressing, learning every subtle curve and dip, every heated inch of skin. Until he was there again, the place where she wanted him to be, with his lips and tongue and hands, and she moaned as he pleasured her, and moaned some more. Heart pounding, spirit soaring, she surrendered to him entirely and came apart in his skillful hands. And then he was sliding up, across her body. She wanted to do the same for him, but it was too late, his need was too urgent, and he was lifting her hips, parting her knees, making her ready for him.

"Let me, Hannah. Just let me," he urged against her mouth.

Knowing she could no longer deny him anything, Hannah opened like a blossom in the sunlight. Sensations swept through her and she arched against him as he joined his body with hers, making love to her so completely and thoroughly she knew she would never ever want anyone else again.

"Wow," Hannah sighed with contentment after they'd both reached a shattering climax. Their bodies remained joined together and he cuddled her close, still stroking her hair. "I keep saying that when you finish making love to me." She pressed tiny kisses into the satiny skin of his shoulder, arm, chest. "But…wow."

Dylan propped himself up on his elbows and looked deep into her eyes. "So you know now, whatever this is," he ascertained softly, "it's way more than a fling."

"Way more," Hannah agreed wholeheartedly.

The question was, what were they going to do about it?

"YOU HAVE TO WORK?" Dylan stared at Hannah over the open engine of a '98 Buick the following evening.

Hannah nodded even as she paused to accept the bouquet of flowers he handed her. It was five-thirty and Slim had already gone home. She and Dylan were alone in her auto shop.

His gaze flicked over her grimy coveralls and the ball cap she had put on backward over her hair. "But it's Saturday night!"

Hannah straightened and tucked her hands in the rear pockets of her coveralls. "I took a page from your playbook and bartered the installation of new shocks and spark plugs in exchange for the installation of my appliances. Which, I might add, should be going on as we speak."

Not quite giving up, he regarded her with wry resignation. "How long is it going to take?"

Hannah shrugged, knowing the best she could do

was guesstimate a time. "Frank Pettrone and I figure we'll both be done around ten tonight." At least she hoped that was the case. Hannah surveyed Dylan's stone-colored summer suit, pale green shirt and co-ordinating silk tie admiringly. "You look nice." Really nice. Nice enough to take to bed right now. Or anywhere else he wanted to go.

He accepted the compliment with a dip of his head. "I was hoping to take you out for a fancy dinner." He looked around for something to lean against, then decided against it.

"Because...?" Hannah asked, her interest caught. She was getting used to seeing him every evening, even as she warned herself against becoming too comfortable with him in her life. She could not begin depending on someone who was only going to leave. Even if he did plan on coming back to see her from time to time, as he had alluded to last night, should they end up in different cities.

Dylan edged closer, smelling like aftershave and the unique fragrance that was him. "Do I need a reason to pamper my woman?" he teased.

Hannah looked down. "That bottle of champagne in your hand says you have one." And she was almost afraid to ask what it was, fearing he had decided to just go ahead and accept the Chicago job.

Dylan smiled broadly, apparently unable to keep

his news to himself a second longer. "I got the announcer's job for the Carolina Storm. Emma's dad, Saul Donovan, called me to his office and told me a little while ago."

Hannah's jaw dropped as she struggled to take in what that meant to both of them. "Wow," Hannah said, feeling genuinely impressed, and happy for him. She started to rush forward to hug him, remembered the motor oil on her, and thought better of it. "Congratulations," she said enthusiastically, wishing she could hug him.

Dylan's grin broadened even more. "So you know what this means, don't you?" he said.

"Ah—" Hannah cautioned herself not to jump to conclusions that might prove embarrassing to both of them. "You'll be on the road a lot with the team?"

"And living here in Holly Springs."

Hannah matched his sudden grin as her mood turned…buoyant. "You going to buy a house?"

Dylan cocked his head, considering. "Actually, I was hoping for a roommate."

Her pulse picked up another notch. Hannah tucked her hands in her pockets again and rocked back on her heels. "Yeah. Who?"

His dark brown eyes twinkled merrily. "Who do you think?" He leaned closer yet.

"You're not really suggesting…" Hannah stammered.

"Why not?" He gestured wide, flowers still in one hand, champagne in the other. "You've got the house. I've got the furniture. With me paying half the rent and utilities, you could get the renovation completed before you know it."

She cast another look at the Buick while she struggled to act as cool as she wanted to be. "Why would you want to live with me?" she said curiously. As if they were simply…roomies. Instead of lovers about to become roomies.

"Lot of reasons," Dylan said, still holding her eyes.

Okay. Hannah drew a deep, bolstering breath. "Name 'em."

Dylan looked as if he wanted to kiss her then and there, grimy clothes or not. "So we could sleep together every night and wake wrapped in each other's arms."

Oh, my. He was back to being romantic again. "What else?" Hannah demanded no less cautiously.

Dylan's gaze gentled once again. "So we could see each other all the time," he told her matter-of-factly. As if his suggestion were the most logical one in the world.

"And that's it?" Hannah said slowly, struggling against a wave of disillusionment. Dylan might not have meant to offend her, but she couldn't help but compare what he was suggesting to the way Rupert Wallace had treated her. Because Rupert too had wanted her around to make life cheaper and easier....

Until he had decided to marry someone else, anyway.

"Convenience isn't enough of a reason to live together, Dylan," Hannah told him sadly, moving away.

She heard rather than saw Dylan put the flowers and champagne down. He laid his hands on her shoulders, guided her around. "But loving each other is," he said softly and sincerely.

Hannah blinked while he simply waited for his words to sink in. "I—you—we never said—" She unzipped her coverall, wanting there to be nothing between them to keep them apart.

"Maybe not in words." Dylan helped her step out of the protective garment, so she just wearing jeans and a T-shirt. His hands cupped her shoulders again, and this time he brought her all the way against him. "But it's been there, Hannah. Since that first kiss." As if to prove it, Dylan bend his head and kissed her, sweetly and tenderly, until her spirits soared and her senses swam.

He stepped back a pace and reluctantly let go of her shoulders, chivalrous to the end. "You don't have to give me your answer now. You can think about it and tell me later."

Hannah surged forward and pressed a silencing finger against his lips. She knew he was protecting his own pride now, as well as hers. But there was no need. "There's nothing to think about," she told him softly, looking deep into his eyes as she wreathed her arms around him. "Because I love you, too, Dylan." So much. "So the answer to our living together is yes!"

Chapter Ten

"Admit it. I was a big help tonight," Dylan chided playfully, hours later, as they walked, exhausted, into her house.

To her astonishment he hadn't merely hung around the auto shop and kept her company while she worked. Instead he had gone back to Mac's, traded his suit and tie for a T-shirt and shorts, and come back to spend his Saturday night helping her work on Frank Pettrone's car.

Hannah unlocked her front door, while Dylan juggled the flowers, champagne and the remains of the pizza they'd consumed midpoint of the evening.

"You were a huge help." Hannah smiled, as surprised about that as he seemed to be. She had never figured Dylan could find the spark plugs in a car engine, never mind help replace them. She led the way inside, flipping on light switches as they went. In the kitchen, the stainless-steel appliances—double wall oven, gas cooktop, and trash compactor were all in-stalled. The dishwasher would have to be put in later, after the plumber came out to finish the kitchen plumbing and install the sink and disposal.

After months of renovation, the house she had in-herited from her grandfather was beginning to look like a home again. And with Dylan there, it felt like a home again, too.

"Are you making fun of me?" Dylan asked, slid-ing the leftovers into the refrigerator.

"No." Hannah cast him a playful glance. "Frank Pettrone already did that."

Dylan's lips curved. "I can't believe I got motor oil on my face."

Hannah studied him with utmost gravity. "And the back of your neck." She rubbed at the spot gently until it transferred onto her fingers. "And right here— under your elbow and across your thigh." She pulled the handkerchief from her pocket and took care of those spots, too.

She enjoyed touching him, even as she took her task very seriously, and felt the change…that resulted in her touching him so intimately. His muscles were hard all over. Anticipation gleamed in his dark brown eyes as he regarded her with a thoroughly male satisfaction and an inner appreciation of her that was daunting.

"You've got a little on you, too," he said, backing her to the cabinets and caging her with his arms.

Heart pounding, she gazed up at him. He looked so handsome and at ease, she wished they could stay like this forever. "Yeah, where?" she taunted softly.

Since agreeing to live with him several hours earlier, she'd had plenty of time to second-guess her decision and wonder if it was the right thing after all. And although part of her felt that she should have held out for a better offer from him—like marriage or at least an engagement—before she made herself so readily available to him, the most vulnerable part of her knew it had been the right decision. Loving each other was enough of a reason to be together. Sharing quarters would only bring them closer. And she wanted to be as close to Dylan as it was possible to be.

He touched her cheek. "Right here."

"Damn." She brought the handkerchief to the spot he had pointed out. "I don't know how I always do that," she complained, embarrassed.

He took the cloth from her and rubbed the spot. "I think it looks cute," he told her, affection gleaming in his eyes.

She rolled her eyes. "Get serious!"

He looked affronted as he straightened away from her and palmed his chest. "Don't I look cute with motor oil on me?"

Hannah flushed as she backed up against the cabinets with the temporary plywood covers in lieu of actual countertops. "Well, yes…"

"See?" Dylan wrapped his arms around her waist and tugged her close, so their lower halves were touching in an electrified line. "The two of us are meant to be."

She could get used to this so easily, Hannah thought as she nestled against the proof of his desire and lifted her face to his. She wreathed her arms around his neck and he lowered his lips to hers and kissed her with a depth of feeling so real, so potent, it was almost enough to make her cry. When at last he drew back, she said, "No one has ever romanced me quite the way you do."

Dylan stroked his hand through her hair. "One part of me thinks that's a shame," he said, taking her hand and leading her toward the stairs to the loft.

"And the other?" Hannah asked while she followed Dylan into the bathroom and watched him turn on the spigot in the tub.

He grinned as he closed the drain and poured bubble bath beneath the running water. "The other part thinks it's great that I'm the first guy to ever really treat you right, because that means what we have is even more special. To you and to me."

He kissed her again, long and soulfully, then looked down at her with such intensity she caught her breath. "You're certainly doing a very good job convincing me," she murmured. Longing swept through her in sweet, hot waves.

"And I intend to do even better," Dylan promised, helping her off with her clothes and into the tub, pausing only to dim the lights and light a couple of candles before joining her in the warm, fragrant bubbles.

"You know, when I bought this tub," Hannah confessed as she gently soaped his chest, "I thought about making love with someone in it. I just never really thought it would happen." Never thought any of her fantasies or romantic dreams would come true.

Dylan took the soap from her and pulled her forward, onto his lap, so she was straddling him. "Well, get used to it," he told her gruffly as their mouths met in another tender kiss. "Because it's only the beginning," he promised.

He skimmed her body with his fingers, filling his hands with her soft, damp flesh. One kiss turned into another and another, until all that mattered to either of them was the desire that coursed through them in powerful waves.

As their ragged breaths meshed, Dylan taught her what it was to love, not just with touch, but with their hearts and souls. He taught her she was just as insatiable as he, that it was better to let their passion build and build before he shifted and made them one. Going deeper, and deeper yet, his fingers moved between their bodies, caressing and loving, enhancing her pleasure. Until the need within her exploded, and he was straining against her, rocking with her, into her. Their hearts thundered in unison as they continued to kiss, their lips locked in a slow mating dance. Lower still, he took her into an even more intimate union, until they could stand it no more, and both of them were soaring, in passion and pleasure, tenderness and surrender.

"WE'RE GOING TO HAVE to tell them sometime," Dylan stated his case matter-of-factly the next morning.

"But Sunday brunch?" Hannah protested, not sure she wanted the opinions of others to influence the happiness she felt. "At your mother's?" Hannah liked Helen Hart—indeed the whole Hart clan—but she couldn't think of a worse time.

Dylan shrugged. The expression on his handsome face became even more determined. "It's the only time this week the entire family is going to be together, so I say let's just do it and get it over with."

Which meant Dylan expected there to be trouble, Hannah thought, reading between the lines.

"It'll be fine," he promised.

But would it? Hannah wondered uneasily, even as she saw there was going to be no changing his mind. He was telling his family his plans with or without her by his side. Now they were a couple, she knew this was something they should do together. So she stopped arguing, put her best game face on and simply went with him.

"I've got some news," Dylan said as the meal wound down. "I'm going to be moving back to Holly Springs permanently and working as an announcer for the Carolina Storm hockey team."

Exclamations of glee and congratulations were heard all around.

Helen smiled at Dylan. She was beaming with pride at his accomplishment. "You're welcome to stay here at the house until you find a place," she said generously.

"Actually," Dylan said, "I'm going to be sharing space with Hannah." Suddenly, you could have heard a pin drop as eyebrows were raised all around. And Hannah knew the fallout from that announcement was going to be even worse than she had expected.

Janey looked at her son, Christopher, and suggested pleasantly, "Honey, why don't you take Spartacus for a walk."

Twelve-year-old Christopher thought about protesting. Then he took a good look at his mother's face and nodded. "Sure thing," he said, accepting the leash from his uncle Fletcher.

The grown-ups were silent until the boy and dog had left. Janey was the first to speak. "I'm assuming there is a romantic element to all this?" she said cautiously.

Dylan and Hannah exchanged looks, not exactly sure how to answer that, or even if they wanted to answer that.

Joe Hart shrugged and gave his brother a searching look. Eyebrows knit together in a concerned manner, he said finally, "Hey. If it makes you happy…"

Fletcher Hart nodded cautiously as he looked at Dylan, man to man. "If you think you've got something there, then you should probably, ah, most definitely, ah, explore it."

Beside him, Fletcher's fiancée, Lily Madsen, made a face at Fletcher's awkward phrasing. "I'm happy for you," Lily told them sweetly, and left it at that.

"Me, too," Joe's wife, Emma, said even more enthusiastically. "I think you two make a great couple."

Mac—the oldest sibling—seemed to feel bound to take a paternal approach, as the male head of their family these days. "Obviously, I want you to be happy, too, Dylan," Mac said firmly. "But just so you know, there's no rush. You can continue to stay at my place as long as you need lodging."

"Thanks," Dylan said drolly.

For nothing, Hannah thought, as all eyes turned to Cal.

Cal shrugged, and avoiding Hannah's gaze altogether, said in an oddly neutral voice to his brother, "I'm probably not the person to be giving advice when it comes to you and Hannah and doing whatever it is you want to do…"

"Well, I for one am not anywhere near that reticent about telling you what's on my mind," Helen

Hart said. She glared at Dylan, all maternal reproach. "I'm tempted to take you aside and talk to you alone, Dylan Matthew Hart, but I can't in good conscience do that. Especially after all your siblings have more or less given you their blessing."

Ah, heck, Dylan thought. *Here it comes.* "I'm sure you do have a lot to say on the subject," he countered affably, aware his plan to announce his intentions to his family in front of Hannah, had been about as wrong as it could be. "But maybe you should spare Hannah the lecture, Mom."

Dylan's mother smiled at him, every bit the steel magnolia. "Perhaps I would hold my tongue if Hannah still had family here, because I know for certain that if Hannah's Grandfather Reid were still alive, he would have plenty to say about this. But since he isn't here, I'll do it for both of us." She narrowed her eyes at them indignantly. *"What are you two thinking?"*

Hannah swallowed and came to his defense. "It's not that big a deal," she told Dylan's mother.

"Yes, it is," Dylan disagreed, letting Hannah know she did not need to downplay their feelings for each other in order to protect him from the sting of his mother's disapproval. "And frankly, Mom, it's none of your business."

"On the contrary." Helen planted her hands on her hips and regarded Dylan sternly. "Because you are my son and because I like to think I brought you up right, what is going on here is very much my business! If you two are that serious about each other, and I can see by looking at you together that you are, then you should be thinking about marriage, not shacking up!"

As much as Dylan would have liked to offer a proposal to Hannah, he knew he couldn't. "We're not ready for that, Mom." He had to know he could trust Hannah completely before he could take that big of a step.

"Will you ever be ready, Dylan?" Helen asked. "Will you ever want to actually make that big of a commitment to someone?"

Now was his chance to tell her—tell everyone—Dylan could see it in Hannah's eyes. Just as he also saw that Hannah thought he didn't have the nerve. And maybe he hadn't, before he had hooked up with her. "I've been married," Dylan said quietly. Ignoring the shocked silence that fell, he continued, "And divorced."

"WELL, AT LEAST YOU TOLD them about your romantic past," Hannah congratulated Dylan the moment they were alone again. "So it's out there and you don't have to worry about them finding out some other way, like your mom did when you lost your job in Chicago."

Dylan shrugged as they walked the shady, tree-lined streets from The Wedding Inn to Hannah's house. He wasn't saying much, but she knew he was exhausted from the lecture on personal responsibility they had both endured from his mother. And the reaction of his siblings hadn't been much better. They had been as shocked and hurt as Helen to learn Dylan had kept so much from them. And although none of them had actually come out and said as much, Hannah had been able to tell they privately had plenty of reservations about Dylan's plan to simply live with her, too. She might not feel that Dylan was in any way taking advantage of her, but his mother sure thought he was. And that hurt Hannah. She didn't want to feel she was disappointing Helen. She liked Helen and had always looked up to her. She wanted the older woman's respect.

"I suppose that's true," Dylan said glumly. "And you're right about one thing. Honesty is always the best policy. Secrets, well, they just lead to trouble."

"Agreed," Hannah said with feeling, wishing she didn't have to keep a single one.

"And now that we're on the subject, anything you want to tell me?" Dylan asked.

Yes. But I can't. Not without permission. But maybe it was time that stopped, too, given how serious her relationship with Dylan was becoming. Hannah paused in midstride as her next idea struck. "I know we had planned to spend the afternoon together," she told him casually. "But do you think I could have a rain check?" she asked, searching his eyes.

Dylan went very still. He did not move his eyes from hers. "Something you have to do?" he asked quietly.

Hannah nodded, wishing she could tell Dylan everything but knowing she couldn't—not yet, anyway—and simply left it at that.

Chapter Eleven

"I thought you'd be with Hannah," Mac said an hour later, walking into his house.

Dylan struggled against the suspicions harbored in his heart, the devastation he would feel if his worst fears proved correct. He didn't like feeling like a jealous spouse, but that was exactly the way he felt right now.

"She had something to do this afternoon." Dylan continued folding clothes and putting them into his bags. He just hoped it was as innocent as she claimed.

Oblivious to the real reason behind Dylan's brooding mood, Mac asked, "Are you moving in with her right away?"

The way Mac was looking at him just then reminded Dylan a lot of his father, and the way his dad had looked whenever he was disappointed in something one of his kids had done. Guilt flowed through him even as he told himself that he was not doing anything wrong here. Mouth set, he turned away from Mac's penetrating law-and-order, right-is-right and wrong-is-wrong gaze. "Looks that way, doesn't it?" Dylan reiterated calmly.

"Hey. You've got no call to be angry with me," Mac chided as he moved away from the portal and out of Dylan's way.

"Don't I," Dylan said dryly. Carrying his luggage out to the front porch, he saw, with frustration, that he no longer had just one sibling to deal with. His only sister had just parked her car and was headed his way, too.

Like his mother earlier, Janey looked loaded for bear. Only, Dylan noted with surprise as she neared, Janey's pique wasn't completely with him. Janey glared at Mac resentfully. "Tell me you're not double-teaming them."

Alarm swept through Dylan. He had no idea what his sister was talking about but he did not like the sound of this. "What do you mean?" Dylan demanded from Janey.

"Isn't it obvious?" Janey threw up her hands in exasperation. "Mac is here with you, reading you the riot act. And I just saw Cal walking into the auto repair shop and Hannah's car parked out front. So what did the two of you do?" Janey stomped up the porch steps to glare at Mac. "Decide you would pick up where Mom left off and tell Dylan to either propose marriage to Hannah, pronto, or back the heck off?"

Hannah and Cal…

Again.

No. It couldn't be. He battled against the sick feeling inside. Then turned to his sister, doing his best to affect an outward cool he couldn't begin to feel. "You're sure you saw Cal over there?" he asked grimly.

Janey rolled her eyes. "I think I would recognize my own brother!"

"Well, don't look at me," Mac interrupted, angling a thumb at his chest. "I wasn't part of any scheme to talk sense into Dylan and Hannah. I just happened to walk in and find Dylan here, packing."

Which meant one of two things, Dylan realized with a sinking heart. Either Hannah had called Cal and asked him to meet her. Or Cal had sought her out on his own, without an invitation. Either way it meant the two of them were together again. And once again, Dylan was the odd man out.

"THANKS FOR COMING," Hannah said when Cal walked into her office at the garage just minutes after she had paged him.

Cal flashed her a grateful smile. "I owe you big. You know that."

Hannah perched on the edge of her desk, as happy as ever to have Cal as her friend. "And the time has come for me to collect a return favor," she replied pleasantly.

Cal scowled, abruptly looking protective. "You want me to tell you it's a good idea to let him move in with you? Because I'm not sure I can do that, Hannah. If my brother loves you, he should be proposing to you."

Exactly what she was thinking, Hannah realized wryly.

On the other hand, just because she was suddenly ready for marriage with Dylan didn't mean Dylan was ready for marriage with her. She loved him enough to give him time. And if he never reached that stage, well, maybe she could deal with that, too. Heaven knew, labels and social conventions had never meant that much to her. The passion and tenderness she shared with Dylan, however, did. And that being the case, she jumped to Dylan's defense the same way he had jumped to hers with R. G. Yarborough the other day. Dylan might not need her protection, but she felt good giving it anyway.

"Haven't you heard?" Hannah quipped, meeting Cal's eyes. "Once burned, twice shy?"

Cal paused. He leaned against the opposite wall, arms folded in front of him. "You knew about his marriage to Desirée before this afternoon, didn't you?"

Hannah nodded, glad Dylan had trusted her enough to confide in her. "He told me."

"Then he must really care about you," Cal offered respectfully. "Because I can't imagine him being at all willing to look foolish in front of you, otherwise."

"He wasn't foolish. He was just misled."

Cal offered a half smile. "Which means you do love him."

"With all my heart and soul," Hannah admitted.

Cal's eyes softened. "Well, good for you," he whispered emotionally. "You deserve to be happy."

"Thank you."

"And so does he."

Glad to have Cal's blessing about that much, anyway, Hannah forged on. "Which brings me to one of the reasons I called you over here. I need to tell him about us, Cal. What we've been doing. Why we've been meeting."

Cal frowned. "You know how I feel about that."

Hannah tilted her head at him. "Now who has too much pride?"

"Touché." Cal frowned, considering. "Does he know anything?" he relented after a moment.

"Not yet," Hannah allowed. "But, Cal, it's there between us. This stuff I can't allude to, and it's tearing me up inside. I want to keep your confidence. I want to be a friend to you and Ashley both, and I want to help you get your marriage to Ash back on track. But I can't do it at the expense of my love for Dylan."

"I understand," Cal said. He took Hannah into his arms for a warm familial hug.

"Do you?" Her arms still wrapped loosely around Cal's waist, Hannah drew back to look into his face.

Cal nodded soberly. "I know what it is to love someone with all your heart," he told her compassionately. "So of course I'll help you make this thing with Dylan work in whatever way I can."

DYLAN WANTED TO TRUST Hannah. He wanted to think she hadn't ditched him to spend private time with his unhappily married brother. But the cold hard facts were telling him otherwise.

He didn't feel good about sneaking up and spying on the two of them. But just like with Desirée, he had to know the truth.

So he walked soundlessly up the stairs and toward her office at the rear of the building. Hannah and Cal were standing in her office, their backs to him. Hannah was talking on the telephone while Cal stood beside her, listening intently. As Dylan approached, he could hear every word they were saying.

"All right then," Hannah said enthusiastically before hanging up the phone.

"Well?" Cal asked her impatiently, as if much were riding on the call.

Her cheeks flushing, Hannah reported in a voice rich with triumph. "R.G.'s coming over now with the cash and the car!"

"You did it," Cal told her proudly.

"No. We did it." Hannah turned to Cal.

Cal held out his arms and she went into them for a hug, as Dylan's heart sank.

"You're something, you know that," Cal told Hannah.

And it was then, as they stepped apart, that Hannah turned her head toward Dylan and saw him standing there in the hall. The color left her cheeks abruptly. "Dylan," she breathed.

Cal looked equally distressed.

Jealousy swept through him, red-hot and ugly. "Don't let me interrupt anything," Dylan said.

Upset at having been discovered like that, Hannah put up both hands in the classic pose of surrender. "It's not what it looks like."

"And what would that be?" Dylan asked, noting his brother looked uncomfortable but unapologetic as Dylan sauntered forward to join them. "Given that Cal is married, you pledged your love to me, and you two were just in each other's arms."

He watched their faces for the slightest show of culpability. To his frustration, he saw none. They seemed as in the dark about what was really going on as he was.

"Not that any of this has seemed to stop either of you for days now," Dylan continued his accusation blindly, wishing the two of them would just confess everything and get it over with so they could all go on with their lives.

"What are you implying?" Hannah demanded, incensed.

Dylan answered her question with another of his. "What are you admitting to doing?"

"I don't know what you think is going on here," Cal interrupted furiously.

He shrugged, refusing to walk away until he had all the answers. "A con job? An affair? Both?"

Hannah sucked in a breath at the venom in his low voice.

"It's obvious R. G. Yarborough is your mark," Dylan continued his observations smoothly. "And whatever you're up to has something to do with commuter flights to Wilmington and '64 Mustang convertibles."

"You were spying on me?" Hannah gasped, her posture stiff and defensive.

Dylan marshaled his feelings into rock-hard resolve. "Someone had to."

Cal stepped forward. "You are way out of line here, buddy," Cal warned.

Hannah pushed Cal aside with the flat of her hand. "I want to handle this."

Cal hesitated. "I don't think—"

Hannah kept her eyes on Dylan's face. "You go meet Yarborough. Do what needs to be done," she told Cal. "I'll take care of Dylan."

Cal scowled and didn't budge. "I don't know if I want to leave you alone with him." Cal glared at Dylan.

"If you're going to defend someone, don't you think it should be your wife?" Dylan said.

Both Cal's hands tightened into fists as his temper soared. "I may have to slug him before I leave."

Until Hannah had come into his life Dylan had never been the brawling type, but right now there was nothing Dylan would have welcomed more.

"Cal. Please!" Hannah insisted more urgently than ever, shoving him out of harm's way.

"All right." Cal went reluctantly. He slanted Hannah a protective glance. "But you page me if you need me," he instructed in a voice heavy with meaning.

She nodded and Cal left.

Hannah and Dylan stared at each other in an increasingly uncomfortable silence. Dylan was aware he had never felt so devastated and betrayed. "So," Dylan said eventually, "this is why you ditched me this afternoon."

"I wanted to meet Cal in private. Yes."

Figuring he'd heard all he needed to, Dylan turned to walk out.

Hannah rushed forward and caught his arm. She attempted to swing him around to face her, and when he wouldn't budge, moved in front of him physically, barring his exit. "Just what do you think is going on here?"

Dylan stared down at the flushed contours of her face, wondering if he had ever really known her at all. "I don't know." He shrugged. "I don't want to think you're carrying on a secret love affair with my married brother, but it's not looking good."

Hannah blinked, suddenly looking very close to tears. "You really think I would do something like that?"

Without warning, Cal was back. He looked more determined than ever. "Let me punch him, Hannah," he demanded in a low self-righteous tone.

Hannah pushed her hands through her hair. She looked as if she wanted to be anywhere but here. "Cal!"

"At least tell him what we've been up to," Cal said after a moment.

Another look of understanding passed between Cal and Hannah.

"I'm not sure I want to now," Hannah said petulantly.

"Well, I do," Cal said, turning to give Dylan another stern assessing look. "I want to see the expression on my brother's face when he finds out what a first-class clown he is being."

Dylan had had about enough of being excluded. "What are you talking about?" he demanded.

Cal sighed, appearing as exasperated as he was angry and insulted. "R. G. Yarborough owns the '64 red Mustang convertible that Ashley and I had our first date in, back when we were both students at Wake Forest. It belonged to a friend of a friend and we borrowed it so we could go out, since neither of us had a car on campus that year."

Slowly, all the pieces began to fit. Dylan's misery increased. "That's why you sent Hannah to see Yarborough at Sharkey's Pool Hall?" he concluded, stunned.

"Yes," Cal snapped.

Hannah got a very peculiar look on her face. "How did you know that Cal— Damn it, Dylan, I knew you didn't follow me there just to get your suitcases out of my minivan!" Hannah said.

Dylan didn't want to admit to eavesdropping, but he knew it was time they laid all their cards out on the table. "I accidentally overheard Cal sending you out to meet him," he admitted reluctantly. "From where I was standing, it sounded like—" He stopped, unable to go on.

"What?" Hannah's eyes glittered imperiously.

Dylan cleared his throat, not sure how to put it. "Like he was your scheduler and you were a hired escort."

Cal let loose a string of swearwords suitable for a men's locker room. "Nice way to put it."

"So you followed me to the pool hall," Hannah ascertained angrily. "To do what—watch? Or see if you could get worked into my 'schedule' yourself?"

Her sarcasm hurt, and so did the truth, because he knew he had desired her even then, even though he hadn't wanted to admit it to himself or anyone else. Because he'd thought—erroneously he now knew—that since she was a mechanic and a chauffeur and a plain Jane to boot, that she wasn't his type. "I didn't want to see you get hurt," Dylan said plainly.

Moisture glimmered in her pretty, emerald eyes. She continued to stare at him disbelievingly. "You really thought I was—that I would—"

Dylan cut short her humiliated stammering, resolved to be as honest as possible. "Yes. No. I didn't know. I mean, the Hannah I knew growing up would never do anything like that. But the Cal I knew would never be running around having secret meetings or sending gorgeous women out to meet wealthy married men in pool halls, either."

"And that's why you made sure you interrupted Yarborough and me that night."

Dylan nodded, proud of that much. It was his only gallantry in this whole mess. "I was protecting you from the creep. The same way I was protecting you whenever he came around to talk to you about Mustangs."

Cal shook his head in derision. "Boy, when you mess up you really mess up, don't you, kid?"

Dylan could see that Hannah was ready to call it quits with him right now. "I did what I felt was right," Dylan continued to explain.

"So you've been spying on me and Cal all along?" Hannah ascertained, determined to think the worst of him.

"I was seeing what I could do to help prevent you

both from messing up your lives," Dylan corrected patiently

"And sleeping with me—" Hannah continued, pale.

"Okay, here's where I exit," Cal said. "For good this time." He leaned over to give Hannah a one-armed hug and a brotherly peck on the temple. "Call me if you want my brother punched out. Although, the way you're looking now, you could probably do a pretty decent job of that yourself."

"No kidding," Hannah said.

Cal left.

She continued to stare at Dylan as if she wanted to deck him. "You really thought I was a hooker," she said furiously.

In retrospect, Dylan was having a little trouble wrapping his mind around the idea, too. He slid his hands into the front pockets of his shorts, more than willing to let Hannah cover this territory again and again if it would make her feel better. 'Cause God knew, he hadn't meant to hurt her in any of this and he had. "More like a con artist," Dylan said affably, recalling how quickly he had dismissed his initial wrong assumption about her being an escort.

Hannah rolled her eyes and stalked away from him. "Oh, that's so much better," she said with a sarcasm that stung. She whirled to face him, her breasts heaving beneath her soft cotton top. "Exactly when did you realize I wasn't a 'con artist'?" When he didn't reply right away, she answered for him. "Not until just now?"

Her incredulous voice ringing in his ears, Dylan thought back to the clandestine running around Hannah and Cal had done, all their secret tête-à-têtes about money, and getting their mystery mark right where they wanted him.

He wasn't going to lie to her. "It all looked pretty damning."

"I don't care how it looked. You knew me. You made love with me! And you still thought I was a cheat in cahoots with your brother Cal!"

Dylan's spine stiffened defensively. He knew he was in the wrong here, but did that mean she should show him none of the compassion and understanding he had tried to show her, even when the situation looked its bleakest? "I never meant to hurt you."

Her face was a polite, blank mask, as if she was hurt to the point of numbness. He knew exactly how she felt. However he had expected this to end, he hadn't thought she wouldn't forgive him or give him a chance to make amends for any mistakes he'd made.

"Funny thing. Guys like you never do."

"I love you." His voice sounded hoarse.

Bitterness mingled with the sadness on her face. "You can't possibly love me. You don't even know who or what I am. And obviously you never have."

"I said I'm sorry," he repeated for what seemed like the millionth time. To no avail.

"And I said it doesn't matter." She sent him a beleaguered smile that matched the turbulent emotion in her eyes as she showed him the door. "It's over, Dylan. The truth is, it never should have started."

Chapter Twelve

"Boy, when you mess up, you really mess up, don't you, kid?" Cal repeated later Sunday evening when Dylan caught up with his brother at Cal's farmhouse, outside Holly Springs.

Dylan walked up to Cal, who was busy applying paste wax to the sides of the red '64 Mustang convertible Cal had acquired that afternoon. "I'm still not completely clear on everything that happened between you and Hannah."

"Then help me out here," Cal said as he tossed Dylan a chamois cloth. "And I'll explain everything."

Dylan picked a place where the wax was dry and ready to be buffed off. "I know you and Hannah were just meeting because you wanted to buy this car from R. G. Yarborough."

Cal nodded as he continued to apply wax to the hood of the car. He regarded Dylan seriously. "But the guy wouldn't even talk to me." Cal sighed, suddenly looking older than his thirty-four years. "I was ready to give up—just buy any '64 Mustang convertible. But when I went to Hannah and asked her to help me locate one that was sound mechanically, she convinced me that my original idea to buy the car that Ashley and I first fell in love in was a powerful romantic symbol of how I would always feel about her." He paused. "Hannah felt if we just had the right approach we would be able to get what we wanted from Yarborough. She sent me to find out everything I could about him while she did the same. We met up to compare notes the night of Janey's wedding."

"Part of which I overhead," Dylan remembered, humiliated to think how he had misinterpreted that conversation.

Cal straightened and pressed a hand to his aching back. "It's just as well you messed up that pool-hall encounter. All Hannah wanted to do that night was get Yarborough interested in her and her auto shop so maybe she could get him to bring the Mustang to Holly Springs for her to take a look at. She planned to figure out through casual conversation exactly what it would take to get him to sell it to me. We already knew pure sentiment wasn't going to work, 'cause I had sort of tried that in my initial contacts with the guy and got nowhere."

That explained the secret meetings and whispered conversations, but there had also been a private lunch in Raleigh and an afternoon jaunt out of town. "You went to Wilmington with her."

Cal looked at Dylan, man-to-man. "To evaluate and then purchase the blue Mustang. We were hoping to be able to make Yarborough a deal on the faster car that he couldn't refuse, and then purchase the red Mustang I wanted, for fix-up, with Hannah acting as the middleman and brokering the deal. And that happened today."

Silence fell.

Worse than the dent to Dylan's pride was the knowledge that he had done the unforgivable as far as Hannah was concerned—accusing her of something he should have known, and in fact *had* known deep down that she was just not capable of doing.

Hannah wasn't going to forgive him for that.

Aware he was dealing with the biggest loss of his adult life, Dylan swallowed. Forfeiting a job was one thing. He could just go out and get another. He couldn't just go out and get another Hannah. There was only going to be one Hannah in his life.

Struggling to contain his depression, Dylan looked at Cal. He hoped Cal had a better result with his woman. "Have you told Ashley yet about the car?" If so, had it helped?

Cal shook his head. "I'm going to surprise her when she comes home, at the end of her fellowship. It's going to be her Valentine's Day slash anniversary present." Cal paused, his determination evident. "Which is why it needs to remain secret, Dylan. I don't want anyone knowing what I'm doing and ruining the surprise for Ashley. All anyone in Holly Springs will know is that Hannah is going to be fixing up this car for a customer as a Valentine's present for a family member."

Dylan finished buffing one area, then moved to another. "You've got my word. I won't tell her or anyone else anything about the car."

Cal tossed another glob of white cream wax onto the trunk and rubbed it in with sweeping circular motions. "Although how you could think Hannah and I—"

"You have to admit, on the surface it all looked pretty suspicious," Dylan defended himself heatedly as he looked his older brother in the eye.

"So why didn't you just come and ask me what was going on?" Cal demanded, looking equally piqued.

Dylan shrugged and rested both hands on the hood of the car. "Because the first rule of adultery is deny, deny, deny," Dylan admitted wearily. "And I didn't want to put you in the position of having to lie to me in order to protect whatever your relationship was with her." He had been trying to save them all further embarrassment. Not that it had worked.

Cal sized him up, looking every bit the caring

older brother now. "You don't believe that line of ma-larkey any more than I do," Cal scoffed, wiping the sweat from his forehead.

Dylan struggled to hang on to the last shreds of his once-considerable pride. "What do you mean?"

Cal looked at him with the cynicism of one who hadn't fared so well in the romance department, ei-ther. "You were just using your suspicion to help you keep your guard up so you wouldn't have to step off the safety of the sidelines and finally get into the game yourself—and put something besides your ca-reer first. But it didn't work," Cal finished slowly. "Did it? You fell in love with her."

"THANK YOU FOR the shopping and lunch and after-noon at the spa," Hannah said as the sleek black limo pulled up to the curb and they all piled in without waiting for the uniformed driver to come back and open the door. "It was really great." Hannah smiled at her three best women friends. In fact, for a few sec-onds here and there she had actually almost been able to have a good time. Which was not an easy feat, when your heart had just been broken all to pieces....

"We thought you deserved some pampering," Janey said, waving the driver, who was hidden be-hind a tinted glass screen, on. "After the hell my brother Dylan put you through the last week or so."

"Yes, well, live and learn," Hannah said, determined to get over the loss of the love of her life if only as a matter of pride.

She had sketched out the reasons for the breakup to her friends, leaving out the parts about Cal's secret purchase of the vintage sports car for his wife, as per Cal's request.

Only to have them all insist she take Monday off and receive some much-needed tender loving care at their behest.

"Although how Dylan could have jumped to the conclusion I was moonlighting as a lady of the evening or some man's mistress or even a con artist," Hannah sighed her considerable exasperation out loud, "I do not know."

"Ah, give the guy a break," Fletcher's fiancée said with an airy wave of her just-manicured hand, and all the romantic aura of the newly engaged. "Not that I'm defending Dylan, you understand, because he clearly was in the wrong here," Lily said. "And, despite all his protestations to the contrary, he has to know that. But speaking as a woman who didn't have much experience when it came to romance—before I got involved with Fletcher, anyway—it's pretty easy to feel unsure of yourself when you're in unfamiliar territory."

And they both had been in unfamiliar territory, Hannah realized. Becoming physically and emotionally and romantically involved with someone they had known from childhood on.

"And given that Dylan had already made one mistake, secretly running off and marrying an untrustworthy woman, only to have to privately divorce her later," Joe's wife said sympathetically, "it makes sense he would have been particularly leery of getting involved with someone he wrongly deduced he couldn't really trust, either."

"Yes, well, he should have known I would never do anything unsavory," Hannah said stubbornly.

"Well, no one says you have to forgive him," Janey said, as in the front of the car the driver suffered a brief coughing fit. "I mean, you could just never speak to him again."

"The only problem with that is, thanks to his new job with the Carolina Storm, he's now going to be living in Holly Springs again," Hannah lamented. "So I am not going to be able to avoid running into him." Or worse, whatever woman he decided to date next. Hannah couldn't think of anything more depressing than seeing him with someone else….

Especially when she was still in love with him and always would be.

Lily studied Hannah sagely. "Well, if it's over and you truly don't ever want to go out with him again, what's the problem?" she said, checking her reflection in her compact. "You don't have to talk to him if you don't want to—just pretend he's not there."

"Yes," Janey agreed as the driver suffered another

brief coughing fit. "Just start dating someone else," she continued. "He'll get the message."

"That's the problem." Hannah settled farther into her seat, her back to the glass partition, and looked at all her friends. "After going out with Dylan, I don't want to date anyone else."

Janey scowled, for the first time looking as if she wished she could shut Hannah up, since she had been talking nonstop about Dylan all day long. "Well, just don't let him know that," Janey warned, completely serious.

"Yes," Emma agreed. "If he wants you back, he should have to work for it."

But would he? Hannah wondered when the conversation turned to Lily and Fletcher's October wedding. Or would he feel, as she did, that her pride had already been wounded enough by all that had happened thus far?

She was still thinking about it as the limo let her three friends off, one by one, until only Hannah was left in the sleek black car. Not bothering to turn around, she pressed the intercom, stated her address and sat back to wait.

Only problem was, Hannah noted some five minutes later, their driver did not seem to know his way around Holly Springs. Because they weren't headed for her neighborhood. "Hey," she said again, pressing the button as the limo pulled up in front of the Wedding Inn. "This is not where we're supposed to be!"

The driver got out and came around to open her door. "Sure about that?" he said, flashing a familiar smile.

THE BREATH LEFT HANNAH'S lungs in a whoosh. "Dylan," she whispered his name tremulously.

A mixture of sadness and wry hope shone in his sable-brown eyes. "At least you haven't forgotten what I look like," he teased, looking as handsome as he ever had on a TV screen.

"Not very likely," Hannah said, her emotions in an uproar. She understood now why Janey, Emma and Lily had been so insistent they all purchase pretty sundresses and put them on before leaving the day spa. Glad she was at her feminine best instead of in work-stained coveralls, with motor oil smudged on her face, she arranged the tea-length skirt over her knees and demanded, "What are you doing here? You don't have a chauffeur's license."

Dylan inclined his head in an exaggerated show of regret. "Tell me about it. I really had to pull some strings to get Quality Limo to loan me one of their cars for the afternoon."

Hannah's spirits rose as she thought of all the trouble he had gone to. But not wanting to make it too easy for him, or take too much for granted, Hannah hedged. She saw now his mother had been right, she hadn't been asking for enough from him. A no-strings love affair had been fine for her just days ago. Now she wanted more. For them to be together, he would have to want more, too. Or at least be open to the possibility. "Were Janey, Lily and Emma in on this?"

Dylan extended his hand. "As well as my mother. Seems all the women in the family think I should make up for my considerable mistakes. And to that end, we have a very special table waiting for us upstairs on the balcony."

Hannah allowed him to help her out of the car. "You're kidding." She stumbled slightly as her heels hit the pavement.

Dylan caught her around the waist and steadied her against him. "I would never kid about something this important," he told her gently.

Silence fell between them. Hannah could feel her heart beating fast and hard in her chest.

"Give me a chance, Hannah," Dylan said softly, brushing the hair away from her face. "That's all I'm asking."

Opening herself up to the kind of hurt she had already suffered from him was a risk, but Hannah knew if she didn't hear him out, she would forever be kicking herself for the lapse. So she took his arm and walked with him up the semicircular staircase that fronted the entrance of the palatial white brick inn, into the grand hall, up the stairs and out onto the private balcony overlooking the lushly blooming flower gardens and manicured lawns.

As promised, they had a table waiting for them. It was set with the inn's finest linens and china. A bottle of champagne was chilling in a bucket. A bouquet of her favorite flowers was tied with a ribbon and laid across her plate. Dylan helped her into a chair, took off his chauffeur's cap and sat across from her.

The irony of the situation, that she had started out driving him and he had ended up chauffeuring her, was not lost on either of them.

"You don't have to stay dressed like that," Hannah said.

Dylan—who looked as sleekly attractive in the black suit, white shirt and austere tie as he did in designer garb—sat back in his chair. "Maybe I want to," he told her. The corners of his lips curved sagely. "Maybe I want you to get a look at me eating humble pie."

Hannah tried but could not stop drinking in the sight of him—it had only been a matter of twenty-four hours that they'd been apart, but she had missed him so much.

Aware humble was not really Dylan's style, she teased back just as wryly, "Is that even possible?"

"For you it is." Dylan removed his cap and ran his fingers through his sandy-brown hair. Swallowing hard, he leaned across the table, took her fingers in his. "Hannah, I'm sorry," he said sincerely. "From the very bottom of my heart and soul, I am so sorry for ever doubting you."

The raw emotion in his low tone caused a riptide of feeling in her. "Then why did you?" she asked.

"Because—" Dylan stood and drew her to her feet, too "—as Cal pointed out, if I let all the reasons why we shouldn't be together fall away, then I would have had to deal with all the reasons why we should," he told her tenderly. "And I wouldn't have been content to ask you to be my roommate instead of my partner for life. But I'm through standing on the sidelines, Hannah, watching everyone else make the great plays." He lifted their clasped hands and kissed the back of her wrist. He wrapped his other arm about her waist and brought her intimately close. "I love you," he whispered as he looked deep into her eyes. "So much that I can no longer imagine my life without you."

Joy bubbled up inside her. "Oh, Dylan," Hannah murmured as happiness welled inside her. She rose up on tiptoe. "I love you, too." Wreathing her arms around his neck, she kissed him with all the affection she had in her heart. "And I can't imagine my life without you, either." And to prove it, she kissed him again, even more thoroughly.

"I was hoping you'd say that," Dylan teased, holding her close and kissing her again and again. "Because love is a very, very important component of marriage and I want you to be my wife," he continued huskily. "So—" He reached into his pocket and pulled out a velvet-lined box. He opened it up to reveal a beautiful platinum diamond ring. He searched her eyes as he asked softly, reverently, "Hannah Reid, will you marry me?"

Hannah nodded as all her dreams finally came true. "Yes," she whispered back. "Dylan Hart, I will."

* * * * *

In
February 2005
Harlequin American Romance presents
HER SECRET VALENTINE,
the fifth installment in
Cathy Gillen Thacker's
captivating miniseries
THE BRIDES OF HOLLY SPRINGS

In this irresistible Valentine tale, the heat is on for
Cal Hart to rekindle the flame with his
long-distance wife! Will Cupid cast a romantic
spell over this troubled duo for a special
anniversary they'll never forget?

Turn the page for a sneak preview of
HER SECRET VALENTINE….

Chapter One

"How long is this situation between you and Ashley going to go on?" Mac Hart asked.

Cal tensed. He'd thought he had been invited over to his brother Mac's house to watch playoff football with the rest of the men in the family. Now, suddenly, it was looking more like an intervention. He leaned forward to help himself to some of the nachos on the coffee table in front of the sofa. "I don't know what you mean."

"Then let us spell it out for you," Cal's brother-in-law, Thad Lantz, said with his usual coachlike efficiency.

Joe continued. "She missed Janey's wedding to Thad in August, as well as Fletcher's marriage to Lily in October and Dylan and Hannah's wedding in November."

Cal bristled. They all knew Ashley was busy completing her OB/GYN fellowship in Honolulu. "She wanted to be here but since the flight from Honolulu to Raleigh is at minimum twelve hours, it's too far to go for a weekend trip. Not that she has many full weekends off in any case." Nor did he. Hence, their habit of rendezvousing in San Francisco, since it was a six- or seven-hour flight for each of them....

More skeptical looks. "She didn't make it back to Carolina for Thanksgiving or Christmas or New Year's this year, either," Dylan observed.

Cal shrugged and centered his attention on the TV, where a lot of pregame nonsense was currently going on. "She had to work all three holidays." Cal wished the game would hurry up and start. Because the sooner it did, the sooner this conversation would be over.

"Had to or volunteered?" Fletcher muttered with a questioning lift of his dark brow.

Uneasiness settled around Cal's heart like a shroud. He'd had many of the same questions himself. Still, Ashley was his wife, and he felt honor-bound to defend her. "I saw her in November in San Francisco. We celebrated all our holidays then." In one passion-filled weekend that had oddly enough left him feeling lonelier and more uncertain of their union than ever.

Concerned looks were exchanged all the way around. Cal knew the guys in the family all felt sorry for him, which just made the situation worse.

Dylan dipped a tortilla chip into the chili-cheese sauce. "So when is Ashley coming home?" he asked curiously.

That was just it. Cal didn't know. Ashley didn't want to talk about it. "Soon," he fibbed.

Thad paused, his expression thoughtful. "I thought her fellowship was up in December."

Cal sipped his beer, the mellow golden brew settling like acid in his gut. "She took her oral exam then and turned in her thesis."

Fletcher helped himself to a buffalo wing. "Her written exam was last July, wasn't it?"

Cal nodded. "But her last day at the hospital isn't until January 15," he cautioned. In a couple of days.

"And then she's coming back home, right?"

That had been the plan, Cal thought, when Ashley had left two and a half years ago to complete her medical education in Hawaii. Now he wasn't so sure that was the case. But not wanting to tell his brothers any of that, he said only, "She's looking for a job now."

"Here, in North Carolina."

Cal certainly hoped so, since he was committed to his job at the Holly Springs Medical Center for another eighteen months, minimum.

"If she were my wife—" Mac said.

"Funny," Cal interrupted, the last of his legendary patience waning swiftly. "You don't have a wife."

"If it were me," Mac continued, ignoring Cal's

glare as he added a piping hot pizza to the spread, "I'd get on a plane to Honolulu, put her over my shoulder and carry her home if necessary."

"That John Wayne stuff doesn't work with Ashley." Never had. Never would.

"Well, you better do something," Joe warned.

All eyes turned to him. Cal waited expectantly, knowing from the silence that fell there was more. Finally, Joe cleared his throat, said, "The women in the family are all upset. You've been married nearly three years now, and most of that time you and Ashley have been living apart."

"So?" Cal prodded.

"So, they're tired of seeing you so unhappy." Dylan took over where Cal left off. "They're giving you and Ashley till Valentine's Day—" Cal and Ashley's wedding anniversary "—to make things right."

"And if that doesn't happen?" Cal demanded.

Fletcher scowled. "Then the women in the family are stepping in."

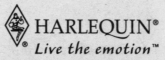

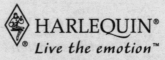

If you enjoyed what you just read,
then we've got an offer you can't resist!

Take 2 bestselling love stories FREE!

Plus get a FREE surprise gift!

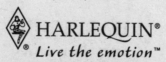

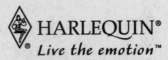